"You fina
I knew y

Mary's sis
making no attemp
welcome. "He's *my* husband,"
Margaret said flatly. "You stole him
from me."

"I... it wasn't that way," Mary
stammered. "You ran off, and daddy
said that I... that he—"

"Don't stammer, Mary. It's all over. I've
come back to reclaim him."

"Margaret, you gave him up!"

There was a tremor in the pit of Mary's
stomach. What had been said was
true. In a way she had stolen
Margaret's husband-to-be. And she
had no intention of giving him back!

All through her years with Margaret,
she remembered, her sister got what
she wanted. But not this time! Not
Harry! *If he wants to keep me,* Mary
thought wildly, *I want to stay.*

Books by Emma Goldrick

HARLEQUIN PRESENTS
688—AND BLOW YOUR HOUSE DOWN
791—MISS MARY'S HUSBAND

HARLEQUIN ROMANCE
2661—THE ROAD

These books may be available at your local bookseller.

Don't miss any of our special offers. Write to us at the following address for information on our newest releases.

Harlequin Reader Service
P.O. Box 52040, Phoenix, AZ   85072-2040
Canadian address: P.O. Box 2800, Postal Station A,
5170 Yonge St., Willowdale, Ont.   M2N 6J3

EMMA GOLDRICK

miss mary's husband

Harlequin Books

TORONTO • NEW YORK • LONDON
AMSTERDAM • PARIS • SYDNEY • HAMBURG
STOCKHOLM • ATHENS • TOKYO • MILAN

Harlequin Presents first edition June 1985
ISBN 0-373-10791-9

Original hardcover edition published in 1984
by Mills & Boon Limited
under the title *Miss Mary's Devil*

CHAPTER ONE

She could hardly repress the giggles as he swung her up in his arms. It was the champagne, of course. There certainly was nothing else for her to giggle about. She was still wearing the mass of satin white that had been her wedding gown. *Her wedding gown!* The restaurant where her father had arranged the reception was only eight blocks away, so it had seemed futile to change there. And now she was paying for it. The dress, cunningly tailored to its owner, was too tight across her more rounded breasts, and it trapped her fuller hips in a vice.

'Well, I'm glad to see you smile,' he said. 'I don't know when I've seen a gloomier bride!'

She stared up into his dark brown eyes. That lock of blond hair had fallen down over his face again, but with both arms full of her weight, he could not flick it back casually as she had seen him do at the altar. She reached out a tentative finger and did it for him. He smiled his thanks, and started up the three white-marble steps that led to the front door of the house on Joy Street. She got one quick look at the house as they moved. It was narrow, unbelievably narrow. There were only two windows on each side of the door, but it towered upward in red brick splendour for four stories, pinned between two massive apartment complexes.

He was panting for breath as they reached the tiny porch. 'Putting on a little weight, have you love,' he chuckled. The door swung open at the hand of a middle-aged, craggy faced woman. He brushed by her, moved into the narrow hall, and set his bride down with a sigh of relief. 'Too much office work,' he laughed down at her. 'I've got to get back in shape. This is Mrs Hudley.' He introduced the older woman. 'My housekeeper, cook, surrogate mother——'

'Come on now, Mr Richardson,' the housekeeper interrupted. 'Welcome to Joy Street, Mrs Richardson.' She extended a warm palm. Mary Margaret managed to grasp it before it disappeared. There was a strange glint in the housekeeper's grey eyes, a wary look. But Mary was too confused, too numbed by the long day behind her, to take notice. Her mind was in a whirl, and underneath the cool exterior she was shaking, fearful.

It had all started when she had left her shared apartment in the village of Beltown at six o'clock in the morning. She had planned to drive into Boston to corner her father, settle the issue of the bills, and be back in Beltown in time for a three o'clock meeting with her new boss, the Headmaster of the village's elementary school. And instead? Bingo! Mary Margaret Richardson, bride!

'Stall him until midnight. It will all be settled by then,' her father had whispered to her at the reception. And then he had patted his inside coat pocket, as if to indicate that all was well with the plan. Stall him until midnight? The huge grandfather clock on the stair-landing was just striking eight. And the blond giant looking down at her five feet four inches of femininity didn't appear to be the sort of man you could stall for four hours! For the first time in this madcap day she took measure of him. A little above six feet, built like a whippet rather than a football player, his gold hair was streaked with white where the hot sun had bleached it out. His well-tanned face housed gleaming dark eyes, sheltered incongruously under thick dark lashes.

'We won't want anything to eat, Mrs Hudley,' he said. 'Why don't you take the rest of the evening off. Everything is all right upstairs?'

'Everything's fine,' the housekeeper responded, 'but I've plenty of food prepared. You sure you wouldn't want a nibble, Mrs Richardson?'

Mrs Richardson. The name kept ringing in her ears. Something to eat. An excuse. Anything to keep from climbing those polished mahogany stairs. Mrs Richardson! I'm married to this man, and I don't even know what his first name is! 'Yes,' she stuttered, 'I am a bit hungry, Mrs Hudley.'

'But you'll want to change out of your gown into something more comfortable,' he insisted. He took her arm and moved her a step or two in the direction of the stairs.

'No, no!' she objected, almost too violently. His head turned towards her, and she could see the question in those gleaming eyes. 'No,' she stammered. 'I—I would rather—I just would like a snack, and once upstairs I think——'

'You're right,' he laughed. 'Once upstairs you'll never get back down again. At least not tonight. All right, Mrs Hudley, you go along. I'll see that my wife gets her snack. You'll come up in the morning?'

'Of course, Mr Richardson.' The housekeeper smiled for the first time, then opened an interior door and went down some steps out of sight.

'There's a basement apartment,' he explained. 'You haven't had a chance to see anything but the bedroom. Mrs Hudley and her husband live downstairs. And the kitchen's this way.' His hand locked on her arm and he began urging her to the door behind the staircase. What in the world did he mean by that, she asked herself as she was being dragged down the hall. All I've seen is the bedroom? What in the world has Margaret been up to? She could feel shivers run up and down her spine again. There was no way around it. She had married this man, and she was afraid of him! And what about her new job? Her appointment with the Headmaster? She had gone off determinedly this morning, set on pinning her father down to a commitment. Set on doing it all by noontime. And now, if she failed to make her appointment? Failed? She was already four hours too late for her appointment, and her new career, after five years of struggling, depended on making a good impression on the unknown Head. She dug in her heels, and he stopped.

'I have to make a telephone call,' she stammered.

'My God! On your wedding night?'

'I—I have to——' She had almost given herself away. I have to, Mr Richardson? Is that the way a new bride speaks to her husband?

'I just have to,' she muttered stubbornly.

'Okay,' he returned, 'so you just have to. Over here in the study there's a telephone. I'll get a couple of sandwiches and bring them over. You want another drink to go with it?'

'Yes,' she mumbled. 'Milk?'

'Milk? What are you trying to tell me, Margaret Mary? You know you never drink milk!'

'Milk,' she insisted, miserably.

'So milk!' He shook his head, and then a grin spread over his face. 'You're not trying to tell me that you're pregnant, are you?'

'Pregnant!' she gasped. Her face burned as she blushed. 'The very idea. How can you talk to me like that?' Her fists balled, and she half-threatened him, before recognising the ridicule of it all.

'Don't bust a gasket,' he returned. 'You know its possible. How many weekends have we spent upstairs in my bedroom these past months? It's possible!' He was laughing now, a full-throated roar of enjoyment.

She turned her back to him, struggling to regain control. The tips of her ears burned uncontrollably. She was unable to stem the tide as huge tears rolled down each cheek. Just as they had done at the altar, when her father, lifting her heavy veil, had dropped it again as soon as he saw the tracks left through her heavy make-up. She shuddered, hugging her fists to her breasts.

'Well, go ahead and make your call,' he insisted. She heard his footsteps, partially muffled by the thick carpet, as he walked towards the kitchen. She began to relax when the kitchen door closed behind him. With one unclenched hand she swabbed her eyes clear, pushed open the door in front of her, and went into the study.

The room was dimly lit by a floorlamp standing near the huge window. The light did not penetrate to the high looming ceiling. For a moment she stopped by the windowseat and looked out into the back yard of the house. A tiny garden, still visible in the late summer twilight, sparkled back at her, an immaculate little place, surrounded by high brick walls.

She turned back to the immense bare desk. An immaculate garden, a clear desk? Is this what he is like, she asked herself? Neat? Compartmented? Why in the world would he want to marry Margaret? Sex wasn't the answer. He seemed to have got all he wanted of that without a licence. Stall him until midnight! How in God's great world could she do that? Her hand fumbled for the telephone, and she automatically punched up the number of the apartment in Beltown. The instrument buzzed at her three times before the receiver was picked up.

'Harriet?' she whispered into the mouthpiece. 'It's me, Mary.'

'Yes,' the voice of her flatmate responded. 'Were you tied up at your appointment?'

'I guess you could say that,' Mary muttered. 'I——'

'Could you speak a little louder?' Harriet asked.

'No!' she squeaked, but she did do her best to speak more distinctly. 'I didn't get to my appointment with Mr Fisher. I have a terrible problem,' she sighed.

'You missed your appointment? Don't you realise that there are ten teachers available for every empty position in this State! And after all the trouble I went to to get you set up in the same school as me!' The voice stopped for a second, and then, with more warmth than before, 'What's wrong, Mary? There's something definitely wrong!'

'I—I went to see my father,' she stammered. 'I told you about that. And he——'

'I see. You let them talk you into something idiotic, did you? Well, when are you coming home to tell me about it?'

'I—yes, he did,' she sighed. 'You wouldn't believe how stupid I've been! And it's not over yet. I just can't tell you—maybe I won't be home until morning. Do you suppose you could—please—tell Mr Fisher I—I had an accident, and ask if I could come tomorrow afternoon? I really need that job, Harriet. I really need it!'

'That's some kind of terrible excuse, but I'll try it on. But you'd better get back here——' Whatever the rest of the conversation was, she missed it. The study door had banged open, and he came in carrying a silver tray. He walked like a panther, she noted for the first time. And he smiles a lot. Ear to ear teeth! The better to eat you with, my dear! He set the tray gently down on the desk.

'Conversation finished? he asked. She stared down blankly at the telephone in her hand. Then, startled, she raised it to her ear.

'I can't talk any more,' she murmured into the mouthpiece. 'Don't worry about me, please.' Before Harriet could add anything she cradled the handset, and sat back in the swivel chair. Her shoulders were squared against the back of the chair, her stomach drawn in, and her hands folded in her lap. Her feet were six inches from the floor. She left them to swing of their own volition as she struggled to erase the lines of fear that furrowed the soft blooming skin of her cheeks. 'My sister,' she lied.

'You were talking to your sister?' he asked in some astonishment. 'I thought you told me you never wanted to have anything to do with her?'

'Yes, well—I thought I should tell her about my wedding,' she mumbled.

'I'm glad to hear that,' he responded. 'I was beginning to think you were carrying on a real feud. Try the sandwiches. Ham or roast beef. And I brought you your milk.'

She manufactured a smile of thanks and pasted it over her lips. Luckily, in the dim light, he was unable to tell it from the real thing. He came around the desk, pulled her wheeled chair back against him. She reacted by reflex, throwing herself forward out of the chair and away from his disturbing presence. 'I think I'll try the roast beef,' she shrilled at him.

He pursued her around the chair, laughing. She snatched at the top sandwich on the tray just as his hands clasped her shoulders and whirled her around to face him. 'I've heard about jittery brides,' he told her solemnly, 'but I never thought to own one!'

Own one? The thought rattled her fears again. She crammed her mouth full of sandwich just as his head lowered towards her. He hadn't kissed her yet. At the church he had turned to her for a moment after the Mass, but with her veil still down he had been frustrated, and other matters intervened. And now, with his face a matter of inches from hers she forced herself out of her hypnotic trance and began to chew. One hundred chews to the bite, that's what Mother had always said. Chew your food, and avoid indigestion! But her stomach was already upset, rolling, still wrestling with the piece of toast she had swallowed for breakfast, and the host of sandwiches and petit-fours she had *not* eaten at the reception. And all of it sloshing around among the dregs of the two glasses of champagne she had been unable to avoid. She gulped convulsively, and brought the sandwich up to her mouth again. Too late.

She found her wrist caught in the vice of his hand. She opened her mouth to complain, and at that moment his warm moist lips swept across hers, gently at first, and then more urgently. Her eyes flew wide open. There had been an electric shock as he touched her, as if a spark of static electricity had snapped between them. The sandwich slipped out of her hand as his tongue probed into the softness of her mouth, and her senses wavered. You're not a kid, she shouted at herself. You've been kissed before! But never like this. Never like this. She fought against the languor that possessed her, pushing against his chest with her tiny hands. The rising tide of emotion that swept her mind obliterated everything she had ever been told, ever read. She felt as if she were drowning, clinging to the topmast of a sinking ship. And then, without warning, one of his hands stroked across her hip, up her side, and under the curve of her breast. Fire shot up and down her spine, rattled through her empty head. Fire and water, incompatible. Except here, except now! Her eyes closed, shutting out the shape of him, leaving only her wild feelings. Her hands had already abandoned her.

Like little traitors they had crept up around his neck, stretching her up on the tips of her toes so she could encircle his strong muscles, and plunge into the tangled curly ends of blond hair that swept down to his nape. His hand dropped to her hip, measuring her closely against him, against all the pulsating male muscles that strewed his whipcord frame. She was floating away from her anchors, floating happily away, cocooned against the wild seas of the mind, murmuring, moaning.

His mouth left hers, sliding down the slope of her neck, nipping at the lobe of her ear, chasing thundering flames under her chin, around the rim of her high transparent collar, and back up to her other ear. Both his hands were roaming now, frantically searching for——?

'Where's the damn zip,' he muttered in her ear. Zip? she could hear an alarm bell sounding in the distance. But no, it was no alarm. A bell. Once, twice—nine times. It struck in her ear like the voice of doom, snatching her back from her floating cloud. She shook her head to clear it, snatched her hands away from his neck, and slipped out of his arms. Nine times. The grandfather clock in the hallway, striking nine o'clock. Stall him until midnight, her father had said. Huh!

She backed away from him, moving around until the desk was between them. He was short of breath, but not from carrying her this time. She was gasping for air herself, breathing so hard that her aroused breasts were heaving against the satin of the dress, where his eyes were fastened. 'There isn't any zip,' she gasped. 'It's all buttons. One hundred buttons. You have to be patient. I'm hungry.'

'Yeah, patient,' he snorted. It took him another minute to control his breathing. Then he collapsed into a swivel chair and grinned at her. 'You must have had your batteries charged,' he chuckled. 'It was never like this before. Eat up. But hurry!'

'We've never been—married before,' she returned. 'I'm hurrying. Can't you tell?' She snatched up another sandwich and began the same routine. One bite, one hundred slow leisurely chews, and a gulp. It looked like fine roast beef; it tasted like sawdust. She sipped at the cool milk, and started again. It was hard going. He sat across from her, tapping one index finger on the arm of his chair, watching her, stripping her with his eyes. He looks as if he'd like to put me between two slices of bread and eat me! What in God's name have I done?

She knew, of course, what she had done. When she had arrived at her father's door at nine o'clock in the morning, she knew. Was that *this* morning? He still lived in the old brick house in residential Newton, one of the rich commuter-belt suburbs that locked the city of Boston into its slums. Nine o'clock, because he had insisted on that time or nothing. It had been four years since she had stormed at him, swept up her invalid mother, and moved out of his grasp to Beltown.

Her mother had lived for only one happy year, leaving behind her a mountain of medical and funeral bills. Backbreaking years, fighting off creditors, living on grants-in-aid, and the tiny salary she earned working nights at the hospital. Long years, as she plugged through the routine of a full-time degree programme at the University, and finally graduated, in debt up to her ears. And during all that time her sister Margaret and her father had lived in luxury in their old home!

'Well, you don't look all that prosperous,' he had grumbled as he led her into his study. But he *had* listened, sitting behind his ornate desk, chewing on a half-destroyed cigar. She watched him as she explained her need. His bluff outdoorsman's image was fading under the weight of a double chin, and his straight brown hair was noticeably thinner. Tall, brooding, not quite overweight, but definitely an apple left on the tree too long, and refusing to admit it.

'But fifteen thousand dollars!' He had whistled in amazement.

'Operations don't come cheap,' she returned. 'And neither do funerals. And neither one of you came. You owe something!'

'But fifteen thousand dollars?' he snorted.

'You've wasted that and more at the race track,' she snapped back at him. 'She was your faithful wife for twenty years. Can you say the same?'

He had the grace to blush. 'I didn't say it was impossible, Mary Margaret,' he insisted. 'I just say that it's a pretty tough sum to get together.'

Her tears were setting him on edge, she knew. He and Margaret were a matched pair. Neither of them ever cried. Or had the slightest thought for anyone else but themselves. He squirmed uneasily in his chair. Something was bothering him. It wasn't his conscience, she knew. He didn't have one. After all he had been driving the car in the accident that left her mother completely paralysed. And not more than three months after her mother had been discharged from the hospital he had moved his current mistress into a bedroom just across the hall. Which was the time when eighteen-year-old Mary Margaret had packed their bags, called an ambulance, and taken her mother away.

He waved his cigar at her as if it were a pointer. 'Times aren't what they were,' he announced. 'Margaret is getting married this afternoon at four o'clock. To a nice man, who is also going to buy out the business. Grain futures are a tough business. Right after the wedding he's giving me a certified check for two-hundred-and-fifty-thousand dollars. A binder on the purchase price. Hmmmm.'

'Right after the wedding?' she had asked cynically. 'It sounds more like you're selling Margaret than the business.'

'Don't be so sarcastic,' he rumbled. 'The wedding is Margaret's business, not mine. You can't sell a daughter these days.'

'You'd sell anything you could get your hands on,' she replied bitterly.

'Don't talk to me like that,' he blustered. 'You need me!'

'I *need* you?' she snapped. 'I wouldn't——'

'Don't give me those old clichés,' he roared at her. He got up, stretched his legs, and walked around the desk. 'Maybe—just maybe—you might be able to do something for me,' he said. 'Stick around for the wedding. I might need you for a few minutes. And if I do, I'll take fifteen thousand dollars of that money and slip it into your bank account. It's still at the First Federal, isn't it?'

'Yes,' she admitted hesitantly. 'But I don't understand—I don't have any reason to trust you, or Margaret either. What possible use could I be to you on Margaret's wedding day?'

He had laughed at her then, with his lips, his voice, his cheeks, but not with his eyes. She had learned over the years to watch his eyes. And now they were cold, dull, hidden.

What could he possibly mean? What could she do that would be worth fifteen thousand dollars to him? It couldn't be some memory of good times past. There had never been any. In all her growing-up years it had always been Mary and her mother on one side, and Margaret and her father on the other. What was it that—and then she realised. This was Margaret's wedding day, and there was not a murmur, not a stir in the house! She got up slowly from her chair, walked over and opened the door. The house echoed with emptiness. She compressed her lips tightly and looked back at her father. He had a sort of hangdog look on his face.

'Where's Margaret?' she had whispered to him.

'She's—well—she went into Boston last night,' he said in a low voice. 'She'll be back for the wedding, of course. She'll have to be!' And the sound of desperation in that last phrase was enough to tell her how she was going to earn fifteen thousand dollars for a few minutes of her time!

'Well, are you going to eat another plateful?'

The heavy sarcasm snapped Mary back to the present. Across the desk from her, her husband was leaning forward, watching her like a hawk prepared to strike.

'Yes. I mean no. I've had all I want,' she stammered.

He got up from the chair and came around the desk. She backed warily away from him, until she was pinned in the corner of the room. His hands reached out for her. She ducked under them, breathing a prayer.

'I'll just finish my milk,' she squeaked. 'If we leave it here all night it will spoil. There's nothing worse than a glass of sour milk to be faced in the morning.'

'Yes, of course,' he had agreed sarcastically. 'What in the world do you know about sour milk? You've never been in a kitchen in your life.'

'I read that somewhere,' she gasped as she sipped at the milk.

He came up behind her, almost encircling her tiny waist with his two hands. 'And that's about enough of that,' he laughed. 'You've got a great Reluctant Virgin act there, but now it's curtain time.' One of his hands plucked the milk glass from her and set it firmly down on the desk. There was too much finality in the act. She dare not argue.

'What—what do we do now?' she asked shyly, and then blushed at her own stupidity.

'Upstairs,' he commanded. 'You know the room. I'll see to the locking up. And by the way, don't open any outside doors or windows during the night. We have a high incidence of burglary in our neighbourhood. I'll be setting the alarms before I come up. You'll have fifteen minutes to get ready. Scoot.'

He opened the study door and pushed her out into the hall with a playful pat on her bottom. She turned right, dragging her feet slowly through the depth of the carpet. He turned left and disappeared from sight behind the staircase. She paused at the foot of the stairs, bemused. He was such a—strange—man. She had no idea who he really was, or what he did, or what he thought, or—anything. But he looked like a Viking in modern dress. And he was her husband.

He smiled a lot. Among his friends at the reception he had been urbane, casual, apparently a good storyteller. While she had been assiduously avoiding him, she had kept a close eye on him. A popular man. And a man of some wealth, obviously.

As much as she was avoiding her husband, her father seemed to be avoiding her. But she finally cornered him. 'Where can we change,' she hissed at him. 'Margaret will want to look well, and I'm beginning to stretch this gown!'

'She's not here yet,' he confessed. 'She's been delayed in Boston. You're doing fine. Keep it up.' And then he had slid away.

A few minutes later she saw her father finally manoeuvre him out of the crowd and into a private office. Barely minutes later they had come out, her husband with a solemn frown on his face, her father with a broad grin of relief. As her father passed her he had patted his inside coat pocket in a pantomime gesture, and given her the 'okay' sign with thumb and forefinger. And in a few minutes he had returned. 'Keep up the good front,' he whispered in her ear. 'I've just talked to Margaret on the telephone. She's on her way. All you have to do now is stall him off until midnight, and she'll be there.'

'And the money?' she had asked breathlessly.

'In the bank,' he said, chuckling. 'In the bank!'

Stall him off until midnight? She had two hours to go, and ahead of her was the narrow graceful staircase that went up to a midway landing where the clock stood, and then turned sharply left to the floor above. I know which bedroom it is? I know beans! I don't even know what your first name is—husband! She had been too strung up during the ceremony to take it in. Weary from the confusion in her mind she hitched up her ankle-length dress and stumbled up the stairs. Fifteen minutes, he had said. Fifteen minutes until—oh lord. I'll fight him off, that's what I'll do. Yes, sure, just like I fought off that kiss. Lord, what a kiss! I never knew that a man could turn me on like that! She had reached the corridor on the second floor, and looked blankly at four identical doors, two on each side, all closed.

The hall was carpeted as thickly as all the rooms downstairs, but she slipped off her high-heel shoes anyway to avoid the noise, and tiptoed to the nearest door. She opened the door and flicked on the light. The room was a large square, outlined in white rugs, white curtains, ivory walls, and two white-covered twin beds. She bit her lip, wondering. No, hardly that. Not with twin beds. He wasn't the type. She backed out into the hall and closed the door behind her. The next door opened on to a larger room done in pastels, blue and gold. And an open door to the rear showed glimpses of a tiled bath. And a big double bed! 'This has to be it,' she told herself grumpily. 'And now what do I do?'

She looked at the two comfortable armchairs positioned by the window, but the bed drew her. She walked over to it, sat down on its edge, and sank into the softness that captured her tired body. Without thinking she leaned backward and fell over on to the bed, with her feet still dangling. It had been a terribly long day—a terribly confusing day, and her long eyelashes were too heavy to hold open. She relaxed, and gradually the outside world faded into the background. Faded, but did not disappear. She could still hear the heavy tick-tock of the grandfather clock, and an occasional whir of tyres on the street outside, but it was all at a distance. She was present in her world, but aloof from it, as if she were an observer on a distant moon, watching through a telescope. Mary Margaret Richardson, wife. It had an odd comfort about it. Mrs Whatever Richardson. He thinks he owns me. He's a devil, an unnamed devil! On the other hand, he looks like a man who would protect all of his possessions. Protect. Cherish. And he promised to cherish *me*, even if I am the wrong girl!

She didn't hear the footsteps. 'What in the world are

you doing in here?' His voice had a lazy laugh behind it that snapped her up.

'I was—I was just looking,' she sighed, 'and I wanted—needed to relax for a minute. I——'

'I can understand that,' he chuckled. 'It's going to be a long night. Come on girl.' He grabbed one of her wrists and towed her out into the hall and up the next flight of stairs. She stumbled after him, half-confused, half-fearful. Up on this landing there were only two doors, one on either side. He opened the one on the left and tugged her into a massive room, big enough to hold all four of the rooms in her flat. Gold was the colour scheme, gold and bronze. And in the middle of the room, holding pride of place, was the biggest bed she had ever seen. He pushed her towards it, then went to another door.

'I'll take a quick shower,' he told her. 'Get ready.'

'Get ready?' she squeaked.

He laughed at her again. 'Yes, get ready,' he repeated. 'We're going to play this game Godiva-style.' And he was gone. She could hear the hiss of water as he turned on the shower. Her head swivelled around the room. Four scattered chairs, a coffee table, sliding doors that could only be wardrobes, and another door, in the opposite wall from the bath. Barefoot, curious, she padded over to it and opened it. A second room was disclosed, smaller, but too dark to see. Dressing room, her mind told her absently. She went back to the bed and sat down.

Why was it, so suddenly, that all her life seemed to be wrapped up in beds? Mrs Mary Margaret Richardson. What a mess! The clock in the hall struck the half-hour. Ten-thirty. Stall him until midnight! Hah! She dropped back on to this bed, as she had on the other. A moment of respite. You need all you can get, girl. You need— and then she gasped. Staring back at her from the ceiling was her reflected self. The whole area above the bed was one huge mirror!

'Oh my God,' she moaned as she rolled on to the floor. 'Surely he's not one of *that* kind!'

'One of what kind?' He had come out of the bathroom wrapped in a light towelling robe. And nothing else, she knew. Nothing else.

'I—I was just—looking at the mirror,' she gasped.

'Oh that! Well, you said you wanted one, so I had it put up. Happy?'

'I—I wanted—oh. I—forgot.'

'Well?'

She eyed him cautiously, backing away to the farthest corner of the bed. 'Well what?' she asked weakly.

He shook his head with a look of mock-disgust. 'You're getting to be more fun than a barrel of lobsters,' he commented. 'Come on, Margaret, we're going to play a game.'

'What—what game?'

'We're going to play the Beast with Two Backs. Hurry up!'

'I—I don't know that game. What do you—what do I do?'

'Come on, lady take off the church clothes.'

'I—you mean—take off my dress?'

'And everything else. Have at it, chum. You know what I like.'

'I—I know—I can't get the dress off by myself. The buttons. They're all in the back. I—maybe I could call Mrs Hudley for help?'

'You don't have to call anyone anymore, Margaret.' He sounded very solicitous. Very solicitous and very wicked. No amount of prayer could make the clock go faster. No amount. She turned her back to him and stood still, her shoulders bent, her head down, a picture of complete dejection.

She could not hear his footsteps, but she felt his hands. They went to her hair, plucking out the myriad pins that had held her long black curls up so that her coronet and veil could be fitted. In a moment it cascaded down around her, framing her heart-shaped face with its border. The hands dropped to her shoulders, then moved to the tiny pearl buttons at her back.

'I don't remember that your hair was that long,' he mused. 'Oh well.' His fingers undid the buttons down to the middle of her back before his patience ran out. 'Damn these things,' he muttered. She could feel his two strong hands sliding inside the dress on to her bare back, and then, with a terrible wrench, he tore the dress down the line of buttons.

'Oh no,' she moaned. 'It was so pretty. So pretty.' She dropped to her knees and tried vainly to pick up the scattered buttons.

'They're only buttons,' he snapped. 'For God's sake get the damn thing off!'

She stood up again, a graceful flawless movement, and the dress collapsed around her, leaving her standing in the taffeta slip which had provided all the rustling noises as she walked down the aisle. He was watching her from a little distance, waiting. He nodded to her, and she knew no further delay would be allowed. Slowly, as slowly as she could make her hands move, she pulled at the hem of the slip and lifted it off over her head.

His eyes followed her every move, gleaming, implacable. She stood still for a moment, hands folded over her breasts, a pleading look on her face. He nodded his head again.

She looked down over her trembling body, clad now only in a lacy half-bra, briefs, garter-belt, and sheer stockings. What an almighty joke! She never wore stockings. Certainly not since tights had been invented. But her father had insisted. She had to wear the whole outfit, for Margaret's sake. For Margaret's sake! Only a quarter to eleven, and she had no more fight left in her. Her face expressionless, she unfastened the garter belt, and using one of the chairs to balance on, rolled down the stockings and threw them into a corner. But when that detail was complete, she could not command her hands to move again. She stood in front of him, shaking so that even he could see.

'Come over here,' he commanded, pointing to a spot directly in front of him. There was a curious expression on his face. She mustered up enough strength to move like a robot to the place which he had indicated. Both his hands came up and cupped her face, forcing her to look up at him. She licked her dry lips and faced him, the tears quivering at the edges of her eyes. His hands slid down her shoulders and rested on her breasts. She was shaking so much that his hands were swaying as they dealt with the front fastening of her bra. As he pushed it off her shoulders she closed her eyes, squeezing them tightly together. She could feel the slight sag as her muscles took up the released weight of her heavy breasts, and then were instantly relieved of the pressure as his huge hands accepted them, caressed them, traced them. She opened her eyes and looked down to where his hands were torturing her. Two huge tears ran from either eye, slid down to her chin, and dropped off on to those hands.

'All right, Margaret,' he said softly. 'What's the trouble?'

She pulled away from him, covering her breasts with her hands, hugging herself. 'I—I'm not Margaret,' she said.

'What the hell,' he snapped, his eyes flashing. 'You're the girl I married. You *have* to be Margaret!'

'I—you know that Margaret has an older sister?'

'Yes,' he sighed, 'I know. Little Miss Prim. The one that ran off with her mother and split the family. So?'

'My—my father thought it would be a great joke to—name us alike. Margaret was christened Margaret Mary, and I was christened Mary Margaret. I'm the older sister. I'm Mary.'

'I don't believe it,' he muttered. 'I don't believe it. You've got a fuller figure than Margaret, and longer hair. How much older are you?'

'Fifteen,' she sighed.

'Fifteen what? Years, Months?'

'Minutes,' she muttered, and pitched forward in a dead faint at his feet.

CHAPTER TWO

When she drifted back to consciousness she found herself lying in the big bed, under a chamois-soft sheet. She was alone in the room. For a moment her infernal curiosity drove her to look up at the mirror. It faithfully reflected the softly curved planes of her face, swathed in a veil of gleaming hair, a face as pale as her hair was dark. A wandering hand confirmed that she wore nothing but her own briefs. Margaret's had been too small for her, and besides, a girl should go to her wedding wearing something old! She giggled at her own imagination, and, trying to muster up a shred of courage, stuck her tongue out at her mirror image. And of course he came in then, carrying a glass.

Her panic returned immediately. She clamped her mouth shut so fast that she almost bit the tip of her tongue. Both hands snatched at the covering sheet, tucking it up under her chin. He came to the side of the bed and sat down there. She tried to slide away, but the tangle of the sheet held her prisoner.

'Your face is all eyes,' he commented. 'Here, drink this down.' He handed her the bulb-shaped glass.

'I—I don't want anything,' she stammered.

'Sit up and drink it,' he commanded. His voice seemed to drop a half-octave when he gave commands. Her hands began to shake again.

'I can't sit up,' she said. 'I haven't—I——'

'Nonsense,' he laughed. 'Here.' He bunched up three pillows against the backboard of the bed, then reached down and plucked her out of her little nest, settling her against the pillows. She snatched wildly for the sheet, barely managing to get it up high enough to cover her breasts. 'Lord, you are a whole lot of woman,' he sighed. 'Drink!'

She shifted her grip so that one hand was holding the

23

sheet up under her chin, while the other accepted the glass. His eyes were shaping her as she moved, tracing every contour of her under the lightweight sheet. She found herself unable to get the glass to her mouth with only one shaking hand. Desperately, she dropped the sheet, seized the glass with both hands, and gulped down its contents. Fire collapsed her throat and burned the roof of her mouth as the brandy slid down to her stomach. A wild spasm of coughing doubled her up and left her breathless.

'Hey, it's only brandy,' he said. 'Don't tell me? Little Miss Prim? You don't drink either?'

'No,' she gasped. 'I—help me—some water, please.'

He ducked into the bathroom and returned with a tumbler full of water. 'My toothbrush cup,' he said wryly as he handed it to her. She was too upset to care. She swigged the water down, putting out the conflagration, then leaned back against the pillows. He stood by the bed, the empty glass in his hand, and a large grin spreading across his face. 'You've forgotten something,' he said. He reached down to where the sheet had collapsed at her waist, and gently drew it up with both hands. His fingers trailed across her stomach and up over her breasts as he did so.

She snatched at the sheet, drawing it protectively tight around her, unknowingly highlighting the shape of her aroused breasts. His eyes noted, but he said nothing. She shuddered again. 'Please—I—please go,' she sputtered.

'Not yet,' he said grimly. 'First I want to know just what the devil went on today. Start explaining!'

'I—I can't,' she mumbled, turning away from him. As she moved she heard the big clock on the stairs boom again. Ten, eleven, twelve. Twelve o'clock. Stall him until twelve o'clock! 'Where is Margaret?'

'I intend to know. Now!' His voice was steel-hard. 'Why did you marry me, Mary?' One of his hands seized her wrist. It was a cool light seizure, bespeaking power and pain to follow.

'I—we——' Twelve o'clock. Surely she had done

enough for the both of them? Whatever she could tell him. 'I—went to my father's house. Margaret had disappeared. My father—he said that she would come back—that I only had to—to stand in for her, and she would come back. I had to do it.'

'Why?' His question was sharp, like a dagger pointed at her throat.

'I had to,' she returned fiercely. 'I needed the money!'

He whooped with laughter. 'So! You needed the money. You married me for my money?'

'No,' she protested. 'It wasn't like that. Not exactly. I needed the money. My father's money, not yours!'

'Well that's a switch,' he said. 'And did you get it?'

'He said he would deposit it in my account at the bank. He said Margaret would be there at the church. And then he said she would meet me at the reception and we would just switch clothes. And then he said if I just stalled things until midnight, Margaret would be here. I'll bet she's downstairs—would you look?'

'There's nobody downstairs,' he reported. He sounded almost sympathetic.

'She has to be. I've got to get back home and—I've already missed my appointment for my new job. I've *got* to——'

'Things have changed,' he snorted. 'Haven't you noticed by now? Margaret isn't coming, and you married me at four o'clock this afternoon. Love honour and cherish!' He walked over to one of the wardrobes, slid the door back, and took out a pair of pyjama bottoms from the shelves.

'You can't—you—I won't let you! Where are my clothes!'

'Don't yell before you're hit,' he chuckled. 'I think I could manage to put off my gross lusts, at least for tonight. Going to bed with you now would be like shooting fish in a barrel. So I'll let you off the hook for tonight, wife. For tonight.'

'But I have to go home. I have to start——'

'Relax, Mary Margaret. You will survive the night, and we'll have a long talk in the morning. Close your eyes. I don't like my women looking at me as if I were a convicted rapist.' Two of his fingers came down over her eyelids, forcing them shut. He carefully re-arranged the sheet around her, tucking a light blanket over all. She mumbled something indecipherable.

'Mary?' he asked.

With her eyes firmly shut she asked, 'Why did you marry me? I mean, Margaret?'

'Now that's my secret,' he chuckled. 'Get some sleep. And don't get any wild ideas about sneaking off in the night. You would trigger the burglar alarms unnecessarily. And besides, you don't seem to have any clothes here.'

'I don't—I——' She sat up in bed, hugging the sheet close. Her shoes were still lying by the armchair, but everything else was gone. Everything! 'You—you lecher!' she snarled at him. He smiled a crooked one-sided smile, tipped a finger to his forehead in salute, and went out, closing the door behind him.

She shuddered under her thin covering, and waited five minutes to be sure he would not return. Then she slipped out of bed and ran to the door. She opened it slightly to peer down the hall. There was nothing to see. The old clock began to strike again. She closed the door carefully, amazed to see how soundproof the room was. As soon as the door latched, the sound of the clock was cut off in mid-stroke. She searched vainly for some way to lock the door. The only sanctuary with a lock, she discovered, was the bathroom.

Mary prowled the room, looking for something to wear. The only item she could find in the wardrobes, besides a double row of his suits, was an old blue bathrobe, whose sleeves were six inches too long, and whose hem dragged on the floor. But it was better than nothing. She kept it on as she crawled tiredly back into the bed and put out the lights. But tired as she was, sleep eluded her. She lay stiffly in the magnificent bed, barely able to control her trembling, until finally, without notice, she succumbed to fitful rest.

Twice during the night she heard noises that brought

her upright in bed. It was not something recognisable, and it had stopped before she was fully alert. She listened carefully, expecting to find *him* breaking into the room, demanding her. *Him?* How I wish I knew his name, she told herself. It's the nameless devil that frightens one the most. The nameless Devil. She dropped back on the pillow, tossed and squirmed, and once again drifted off. But the third time she heard the noise it was no longer a phantom. As she sat up in her bed it continued. It was not particularly loud. A soft whimper, but monotonously continued, and definitely coming from the quiet dark room which she had previously assumed was a dressing room.

Mary snapped on her bedlight, swung her feet out on to the thick rug, and padded silently over to the half-opened door. As she pushed her way into the adjoining room the noise became louder. She fumbled around in the darkness until she saw a lamp outlined against one of the windows. She padded carefully over to it, and snapped the switch. The small glow of light centred on a dark green rug at her feet, but the noises were coming from behind her. She turned quickly. Against the wall a small trundle bed sat, and under its green and gold covers, a tiny body was outlined.

She walked over to the bed, but nothing could be discerned. Slowly, gently, she pulled off one of the pile of pillows at the head of the bed, and there suddenly she had her answer. Not the answer to what was causing the noise, but rather the answer to the question as to why *he* wanted to marry Margaret! Lying flat on the bed was a tiny elfin face, almost surrounded in swathes of long golden hair. A little girl, perhaps seven or eight? Mary could not be sure. Her life had not included small children, but this one grabbed at her heart.

There was a tiny blush of red at the centre of each of the soft round cheeks. Long dark eyelashes curled over sparkling eyes. The mouth was half open, as if the child were having trouble breathing through her nose, and a gap in front demonstrated that most of her baby teeth had gone. Mary had expected shock, screams at the invasion by a stranger. But that was not what she got. Two deep blue eyes blinked, seemed to focus on something in the distance, and the golden head was cocked to one side, listening.

'Is anyone there?' The voice was high but musical, soft but clear.

'Here,' Mary said quietly, and moved up to the side of the bed. The golden head swung in her general direction, and a hand reached out and touched gently on her wrist.

'Are you my new Mommy?'

'I—I think——' Mary stuttered.

'It's all right,' the little girl responded. 'Daddy told me. But you're not the same one. I was dreaming about you, I think. You sound so much prettier. Much!'

'Much prettier than what?'

'Much prettier than that other one who came. I like you. I need to go to the bathroom.'

'I like you too,' Mary chuckled. 'What in the world is your name?'

'My for-real name is Jennifer. Jennifer Richardson.'

'So they call you Jenny?'

'Nope. When I was little I couldn't say the Jay sound. They call me Penny. I'm eight years old, and I really have to go.'

'So all right, Penny. Up you come. The bathroom's empty.'

The little girl slid out of the bed, shaking down her long nightgown so that it reached to the floor, and then stood there, waiting.

'You have to hold my hand, you know,' the child said. She raised her right hand.

'Oh? Well, all right.' Mary stretched out her own hand, but the child made no movement to meet her. Puzzled, Mary moved her hand the rest of the way, clasped the tiny fingers, and gave a tiny tug. The girl smiled sweetly, tightened her grasp, and began to walk straight ahead, directly into the big armchair that sat by the bed. Barely in time Mary pulled her aside, knocking her off-balance. The child stumbled, fell against Mary's leg, and circled it with both arms.

'I don't know this room very well,' the child said. 'And I think Daddy must have moved his chair.' She turned her head up towards Mary and smiled an angelic smile.

Beautiful teeth, Mary thought, examining the pixie face closely. Plump cheeks, rose-red, coming down to a narrow chin. Golden hair, molten gold, tumbling down to her waist. Long curling eyelashes, two shades darker than her hair. Blue eyes, deep cerulean blue, that sparked in the light from the adjacent room, but whose pupils did not sparkle with the added light. Beautiful blue eyes—that saw nothing.

Mary drew in her breath, barely a sounded gasp, but the little girl heard. 'Did I spoil it?' the child asked. 'Daddy didn't want to tell you because he said you might not come with us if you knew I was blind. Did I spoil it all?'

'No,' Mary said comfortingly. 'You didn't spoil it. I could love you just the same, if you would let me?'

'I want you to—ah—do I call you Margaret? That's what Daddy said. Or can I call you Mommy?'

'You may call me by my name if you like. But my real name is Mary, not Margaret.'

'But Daddy said Margaret Mary is what they called you.'

'Your daddy got it a little twisted, dear. It's Mary Margaret. Okay?'

The trip to the bathroom was somewhat perilous. The little girl provided careful coaching, but Mary's hands were all thumbs. But at last, full of laughter, they were back in the big bedroom, heading for the door of the smaller room.

'Mary?' The little figure stopped, halting them both in place.

'Yes?'

'Daddy's not here?'

'Not right now, pet.'

'Are you going to sleep in that great big bed all by yourself?'

'I—I guess I have to.'

'I 'spect you'll be awful lonesome there by yourself?'

'Yes I will, dear. What can I do about it?'

'Well, you've been so nice to me and all, I guess I could sleep out here with you and keep you company. Would you like that?'

I know who your father is, Mary whispered to herself. I know who your father is, little girl. And I'd better be careful of you both! But her heart wasn't in the argument. 'That would be nice,' she agreed. And so when next she settled into the bed there was a little warm bundle cuddling close to her, squirming around until the blonde head rested on Mary's shoulder.

'Mary,' the girl whispered drowsily in her ear, 'you're a lot softer than my daddy.'

'Well I should hope so,' Mary chuckled into the darkness, just before they both fell into a deep sleep. When the bedroom door opened at seven they were still sound asleep. The man standing in the doorway studied them for a few minutes, caught by the tangled frame of soft golden hair intermingled with the dark sheen of curls, the little head so trustingly laid on the shoulder of the woman he had married.

'Thank God,' he whispered to himself. 'I think I've just been saved from a terrible mistake.' He shut the door behind him, and hurried off to do the critical things he knew must be done.

Mary was just coming back from the bedroom two hours later when she noticed the hand reaching out, the blonde head turning from side to side, listening.

'I'm here,' she said softly. There was the sound of warm welcome in her voice, and it brought an instant smile to the child's face.

'I thought maybe I dreamed it all up,' Penny admitted. She sat up, hugging her knees to her chest. 'It was such a wonderful dream—Mary?'

Mary moved closer to her, and the child's hand touched her robe. 'You don't got no nightgown?'

'I'm real, all right,' Mary laughed, 'and no, I don't

got no nightgown! Do you realise it's nine o'clock? Out you come, and let's get down for some breakfast.'

Twenty minutes later they arrived hand in hand at the kitchen door. 'Ah, there you are,' Mrs Hudley commented. 'It's not very often that Penny stays in bed later than seven o'clock. Did you have a good sleep, baby?' She ran an affectionate hand through the long blonde hair.

'The best I ever had,' the little girl exaggerated. 'It's nice sleeping with Ma—Momma.'

The housekeeper looked at Mary over the child's head. There was a speculative look on her face, quickly replaced. 'There's breakfast in the kitchen, or in the dining room, Mrs Richardson.'

'In the kitchen, of course. And please, call me Mary.'

'Mary? I thought that—he did say Margaret, I'm sure.'

'Of course it is,' Penny interjected. 'Her name is Mary Margaret.'

'Oh? That's the way of it, is it. Well then, into the kitchen we go.' As Penny scrambled in ahead of them, the housekeeper said softly, 'She doesn't make friends very easily. But then, you've met her before, I suppose?'

Mary smiled and shook her head. 'I've never been here before,' she returned, and walked through the door.

The kitchen was a surprise. Like the other rooms in the house it was longer than it was wide, and totally white. A large kitchen table stood in the middle of the floor, while every work-saving gadget that ingenuity could provide was lined up around the perimeter walls.

'And you make all this go?' Mary asked.

The housekeeper laughed at her amazement. 'Not me,' she chuckled. 'Himself. He buys everything in the world that he hears about. Wants to keep me sweet, he says. Good cooks are hard to find. I don't ever touch any of those fancy goods. I use this gas cooker over here, and that microwave oven over there, and that's about it. Here, take a seat. Bacon and eggs today. Coffee?'

Throughout the slow and leisurely breakfast Mary did her best to pump her two companions about this new husband of hers, with little success. He was, she learned, an investment banker, a small-boat enthusiast, an airplane pilot, and 'a devil with the ladies!' This last bit, accompanied by laughter, from Mrs Hudley. Mr Richardson was, Mary concluded, the soul of kindness and discretion. His daughter loved him. His housekeeper loved him, and—but *that* thought was too foolish to be entertained. She banished it quickly, and tried another subject. When prodded, Penny said, 'I call him Daddy. Mrs Hudley calls him Mr Richardson. And there's a whole bunch of people where he works, and they all call him sir.' Which seemed to be about the end of *that*!

She was on her third cup of coffee when the huge clock on the stairs recalled her to reality. Ten-thirty? How in the world could she rescue her position with Mr Fisher? There just *had* to be some way to get herself clothed and on the road to Beltown.

'Mrs Hudley,' she started to say, 'I have to find some clothes so I——' and at that moment *that man* stomped into the kitchen, both arms laden with packages.

'Daddy!' the little girl screeched as she climbed out of her chair. She stood expectantly beside the table, arms upraised. Her father crossed the room in three giant strides, dropped the packages on the table, and swept her up in a mighty hug.

'Well now, baby,' he said. 'Did you enjoy your present?'

'Wonderful,' the child squealed. 'Wonderful! And she's so soft and nice. Not like that other one.'

'Squeezable, huh?' he returned. 'I must try that myself pretty soon.' His eyes were hard on Mary as she blushed and tugged the loose ends of her robe tighter.

'But I don't know what to call her,' the child continued.

'Well, that's easy,' he said, tossing the child up towards the ceiling. 'You call her Mama, or Mother, or whatever.'

'But—I——' Mary stuttered.

'Finished your breakfast?' he interrupted. 'Mrs Hudley, I have to talk to my wife for a few minutes. Could you bring us more coffee in the study? And you, little bit, you scoot into the library and do your Braille reading. Pronto!'

Nobody seemed ever to argue with this man, Mary told herself. They just smile as if *they* had thought of the idea, and—and here I am following him down the hall as if he were my lord and master!

'In here, Mary,' he ordered as he opened the door. His hand was warm against the middle of her back, urging her gently forward. She struggled to snatch at the last shreds of her independence.

'You can't do that,' she said as soon as he closed the door behind them. 'You know this is only a temporary arrangement. I'll be out of your life in just a few hours, and you will cause the child all sorts of problems when she tries to adapt to Margaret. We're not the same kind of people, you know.'

'Oh, I know,' he laughed. 'I know.' He walked around the desk and sank into the swivel chair with a sigh of relief. 'I hate to run around so early in the morning,' he complained.

'Run around?' And the moment the words were out of her mouth she cursed herself. She didn't want to know! Inordinate curiosity, that was her main failing in life. And it always led to trouble.

'Yes,' he laughed. He leaned back against the strength of the springs in the chair. 'It's too far to Beltown for me to go out for your clothes. But I did call from your father's house. Harriet, is it? She said she'd be delighted to pack everything for you. And Mr Hudley is on his way out to get them now. In the meantime, I brought you a few things. Where did I leave the packages?'

'In the kitchen,' she snapped. 'What do you mean, you called Harriet—and my clothes—and how did you know?'

'I went over to your father's house and asked the housekeeper for your address,' he chuckled. 'They were all packing up over there. It seems your father sold the house. It's all elementary, my dear Watson. Oh, by the way, I also called the elementary school and told them to cross you off their list.'

'You what!' she screeched at him. 'You——' Words failed her for the first time in her life. She slammed her fists on the desk top in frustration. 'Four years I've worked to get my teacher's degree,' she finally managed to get out. 'Four years of slaving and half-starving. I *need* that job. I *want* that job. You big overgrown—oh, now what am I going to do? What did you tell them?'

'I told the Head that you had caught a terminal case of marriage. He seemed to think it a very adequate explanation.'

She could not hold back the tears. They flowed like two big rivers down each cheek as she stood there in front of him, flatfooted, arms down at her sides, fists clenched. He was up out of the chair before she saw him move. His two big arms wrapped themselves gently around her, pulling her against the softness of his cardigan.

'There, there now,' he muttered into the crown of her hair. One hand gently patted her shoulder. It was all so comforting that she let herself go, leaning against the strength of him, letting the cleansing tears run for all they were worth. When the tear ducts were empty she sniffed a couple of times, and found that his handkerchief was drying her cheeks. Both of her arms, for some reason beyond her ken, had twined themselves around his waist, squeezing her against him more closely than before.

'You're tired,' he said softly. 'It's been a long hard struggle, with lots of confusion. But it's all over, Mary. All the heartaches, all the loneliness, all the fighting. From here on in I'm going to take care of you. Relax.'

She could almost believe him. It *seemed* to be all over. It seemed as if the terrible years were behind her, and there was refuge in these strong arms. But then she remembered that it was all for Margaret, and the daydream faded.

'We're not really married,' she sighed into his sweater, 'so nothing's changed. Margaret will be coming today, I'm sure. Daddy said she would come last night. I'm sure it's only a little mix-up.'

Instead of answering he swept her up in his arms and carried her over to the large armchair by the window. He sat down, holding her on his knees with a familiarity that made it all seem to be right. And then he gave her the first of her shocks of the day.

'Don't count on Margaret coming,' he chuckled. 'She left for England on PanAm flight 192 yesterday afternoon.'

'Oh that's nonsense,' she started to say, but deep in the back of her mind that nagging conscience was saying 'you know it's true, don't you, sucker!' She pulled herself away from his too-comforting chest and crossed the room to another chair, trying vainly to keep the flaps of her robe closed.

'You bargained for a wife,' she said primly, 'but not for me. I intend to get myself dressed and out of here this morning, Mr—what the devil is your first name, anyway?'

'What the devil is my name?' He lay back his head and roared with laughter. 'You married me, and you don't even know what my name is? Harry. Harry Oscar Richardson.'

'Well, Harry whatever, it was Margaret you married, not me. I distinctly remember that at the altar. Will you, Margaret, take——'

'Ah, but you didn't keep your cool, did you,' he laughed. 'I went over to Saint Anselms this morning and checked the Register. And how did you sign it? Mary Margaret McBain. As big as life!'

'I didn't!' It was more like a prayer than a statement.

'So I rounded up the pastor, and explained the error he had made in the marriage certificate, and he corrected it on the spot.' He reached into his sweater pocket and brought out an official-looking paper. She waved it away, dazed. There was so much of finality, of rock-solid officialese about the whole thing. You are married to him, it screamed at her. There's no way to get off the hook. In the sight of God and Man!

'But it can't be legal!' She returned to the fray, desperate to find a loophole. 'You meant to cheat Margaret all the way, didn't you! That makes it illegal!'

'What the devil do you mean by that?' he snapped.

'You know what I mean,' she snarled. 'You wanted a mother for your daughter.'

'Of course I did. That was the bargain.'

'But you never told Margaret that your daughter was blind, did you! Did you?'

'How about that,' he chuckled.

'You knew that Margaret didn't like children, and a blind child at that. That's cheating. That's despicable! And I'll bet that's illegal, too!'

'Whoa now,' he said, a sombre expression flashing across his face. 'The McBains are talking to me about honesty? You married me for money. Your sister skipped out on a promise, and your father has been running a confidence game for the past year. How about that! Don't you know why your father wanted you to stall me until twelve o'clock last night, you silly goose?'

'No, I don't,' she admitted with abject candour.

'Let me tell you about McBain Grain factors,' he said gruffly. 'A year ago your father leased one storage warehouse, filled it with grain, and then got a bank to give him a full-value loan on the grain. After the bank had inspected the warehouse and sealed it, he broke the seal, leased another warehouse, and moved the grain from the first to the second one. Then he forged a seal on the first warehouse, and went out to a different bank for a full-value loan on the second one. And he's been doing that for a full year. McBain Factors now hold leases on sixteen warehouses, but only one of them has any grain in it. Last month the banks started to make inquiries, along with the Department of Agriculture. So your father arranged to sell me his share of the business, along with Margaret.'

'You can't sell daughters on the open market,' she protested feebly.

'The hell you can't. And you know what else happened?' She looked at him mutely, her eyes dark-shadowed. 'Last night your father took all his liquid assets, my check for two-hundred-and-fifty-thousand dollars, and all his luggage, and boarded the midnight flight to Columbia, South America. How's that for honest?'

'My daddy wouldn't—why Columbia?'

'Because it's the only major country in the western hemisphere which does not have an extradition treaty with the United States!' He walked over to her chair, placed a hand on each arm, and leaned over to kiss her forehead. He was smiling. Grinning!

'You're not angry?'

'Of course not,' he chuckled. 'I always use a long spoon when supping with the devil.'

'I don't understand,' she sighed, all her strength and defiance gone.

'Neither does your father,' he returned. 'I happen to have just financed a company which purchases grain for shipment to Egypt. They have everything they need to make a good profit, except for storage warehouses at shipping points. Now, McBain Factors goes into bankruptcy tomorrow, leaving me with first lien on what? Sixteen empty grain warehouses!'

'Why—why you're as bad as my father,' she snapped.

'Worse,' he chuckled. 'But my deal is legal. If the FBI catches up with your father he'll spend a considerable time in prison. Publicity in all the newspapers, of course, and on television, everything. How would you like that?'

'You mean if I agree to remain with you, he wouldn't have to go to jail?'

'There's always that,' he chuckled. 'You're a devil of a better bargain than Margaret, believe me!'

'Well, that horse won't run, Harry Richardson. If I thought you could hound my father to jail I'd stand on the sidelines and cheer you on. Want me to call the

District Attorney for you?' She tried to stand up to reach the telephone, but he pushed her gently back into the chair.

'No,' he said softly, 'I don't want you to call the District Attorney. If you want to call somebody, call your bank.'

'My bank? Oh! You mean he didn't deposit the money for me?'

'Of course he didn't. Are you that much of a simpleton?'

'I—I guess I was, wasn't I,' she said morosely. 'And now I don't even have a job to help pay off the debt!' She settled back in the chair, her fingers twisting in her lap. He used one big hand to still hers.

'What kind of bills are they?' he asked.

'Just two,' she sighed. 'Four thousand dollars for mother's funeral, and eleven thousand dollars in hospital bills for her last illness.'

He straightened up and glared at her. The mood change sent her deeper into the chair. She brought her hands up in front of her face for protection. 'Why that bastard!' he muttered. 'That rotten bastard!'

He turned away from her and paced slowly up and down the length of the room. She watched him from the corners of her eyes, not daring to turn her head. In anger he was a fearsome thing! When he came back, he leaned over her again, supporting himself on the chair arms.

'There are a lot of reasons why we should be married,' he said softly. 'I need a wife. Penny needs a mother. You and I both want to keep your father's peccadilloes out of the paper. And you need money to pay your debts. Isn't that enough to begin with?'

'You mean—you would pay the bills? If I——'

'You don't expect me to have my wife hounded by bill collectors do you? What I have I protect.'

'I—but you know—I don't love you. I'm not even sure that I like you. I could be a mother for Penny, and run your house, and be your hostess, but—I couldn't— I couldn't be a real wife to you. You know that!'

'You forget one important thing,' he said softly.
'What?'

His lips zeroed in on the tip of her upturned nose, and gently deposited a kiss. 'At four o'clock yesterday afternoon,' he continued, 'at the altar of Saint Anselms, you promised in the sight of God to love, honour, and cherish me. You said that, Mary, not Margaret. You. Do you mean to break that oath—so soon?'

She stared up into his deep star-flecked eyes, so close that she could see nothing else of his face. In the depths of her mind she could hear the echo of the old priest's cracked voice: 'Do you—love, honour, cherish—till death do you part?' You gave your word, Mary! And now it's time for the pledge to fall due! She searched his eyes again, looking for hope, for pity, for forgiveness, and found nothing. She squeezed both her eyes shut.

'No,' she said, 'I have no intention of breaking my oath.' She wanted to say something more. A million more things about doubts and limitations and safeguards, but his lips moved to hers, sealing her mouth as well as her mind. And in a moment he had transported her to the realms of light.

CHAPTER THREE

HE was gone by one o'clock, and when the door closed behind him Mary felt that she had just survived a hurricane. Even Penny was impressed. 'He don't usually go so fast,' the little girl said. 'Did you get your 'structions?'

Mary looked down at her, startled. 'Yes,' she admitted, 'I guess I got my instructions. You too?'

'Yes,' the child returned. 'He told me I gotta—I have to look after you, cause you're a babe in the woods. What does that mean?'

'I haven't any idea,' Mary giggled. 'Are there any woods around here?'

'I don't know neither. I've only been here a year, you know, and the rest of my—the ladies, they never took me noplace. Could we go someplace?'

'Why of course we can. Anywhere special?'

'No, just someplace else, please?'

'You bet. Wipe your chin, you've got egg salad on it. You won't need a sweater. We'll go for a little walk through Beantown.'

'My, you are funny. Beantown?'

'You bet. Boston has a million names. Bean Town, because of Boston Baked Beans. Or the Hub, because it's the Hub of the Universe as far as culture goes. How about that?'

'Don't nobody just call it Boston?'

'Sure. The mayor and the tax collectors, and such like!'

'I gotta take my cane. You gotta find it, Mary. They said I always have to take my cane so people would know that——'

'Do you want people to know?'

'No—No, I don't, but Daddy said——'

They were out the front door before Mary regretted

the words she had used about 'Daddy said'. Penny laughed all the way. 'Sometimes I think you don't like my daddy,' she squealed.

'Sometimes I think I don't either,' Mary mumbled under her breath. 'Take my hand and hold tight, because here we go.'

They both had to lean forward to top the hill as Joy Street led into Beacon Street. As they walked Mary kept up a continuous chatter describing everything they passed, everything that moved, everything that had a fragrance. It was the little things that affected her, brought tears to her eyes. When they passed the little red fire hydrant just up the street from the house Penny insisted that they stop so she could 'see' it with her hands.

'It's just like I remembered,' the little girl gasped. 'Is it red, or what?'

'It's red,' Mary assured her, 'with some yellow on the places where the hoses fit. Mickey the Squirter we used to call them when I was young. You've seen one before, Penny?'

'Oh yes, before I was blind. But I was little then. Four years old, I think.'

'Oh? Back when you were young? What happened?'

'Well, we didn't live here then, you know. We lived in New York. And Mommy—my other mommy——'

'Your real mommy, poppet. Don't be shy about the words.'

'She don't seem as real as you are, Mary Margaret.'

'Thank you, fair maiden,' Mary laughed. 'And what happened?'

'I—I don't remember everything. Mommy took me in the car. She was mad. She said we was gonna go live with Grandma. Then we had this accident, you know, and Mommy got dead and I got blind. And when Daddy came he was mad! Lordy how mad he was. He said a lot of bad words, and then I don't remember. Did you ever have a accident?'

'Not that I remember, but it could happen to anyone.'

'I don't think so. Daddy said it could only happen to drunken fools. I don't know who that was. What do you think?'

What I think, Mary told herself, is I've got to stop listening to tales about his first wife. If he wants me to know he'll tell me. And if he finds out I've been pumping his little girl it'll rain for forty days all over my head!

'I think we'd better turn up Beacon Hill, honey. Hear all that noise? Something's going on at the State House.' As they strolled up the pavement together she described in detail the capitol building of the State of Massachusetts, set back from the sidewalk by multiple flights of gleaming stairs. Red brick, with white facings, and a gaggle of plain white columns standing marshalled across its front. A huge building containing both the legislature and the executive offices of the governor.

'And up there on the top—you'd never believe it, Penny!'

'What?'

'They have a big gold dome. At least it looks like gold. Maybe it's only gold paint—but it shines in the sunlight, and sparkles like anything!'

'It must be very important?'

'Very important. The men and women who come to work in this building make all the laws of the State. They call it the Great and General Court of the Commonwealth of Massachusetts.'

'Wow! That's a lot of words!'

'Not as many as they use inside!' There was a crowd gathering in front of the State House, opposite sides of some public argument. 'Let's go up the steps and get back in a corner, sweet. There's quite a crowd collecting! Maybe this isn't the best idea I ever had!' *Maybe* it isn't I'll run home and tell my—that man— that I lost his little girl on our first day out? What a reception that would get! Why do I act as if I were frightened half to death of him? Because it's true?

'Who is making all that noise, Mommy?'

'There are two groups of people, dear. They've come to let the legislature know what their opinion is about a—oh my—about a thing called ERA. The ones on your right hand are for it, and on your left hand they're against. And there are six policemen on horses between the two groups.'

'And they're yelling at each other? I bet that's fun!'

'I'll bet it is too,' Mary sighed. 'I wish I had the nerve to do it.'

'Why don't the policemen tell them all to go home?'

'Because they have the right to be heard, dear. As long as nobody throws anything, or starts a fight, the policemen are going to let them have their say—oops. That did it. Somebody threw a rock. Back up the stairs, Penny. Here, we'll duck behind this column! Keep your head down, baby!' My God, what have I done now, she asked herself as she huddled over the girl, trying to protect her with her own body. The very first time she's in my charge, and I get her mixed up in the middle of a riot! If the child get's frightened, he'll beat me half to death when I get back home! Back home? What a strange thought!

She stooped to bring Penny closer, scooping her up for face-to-face contact. But the mobile little face pressed close to hers was far from fright. Mary took a deep breath for the first time in many minutes. Penny's mouth sparkled with giggles as she pressed her little blonde head close to the raven curls of her new mother. 'I never had so much fun in a long time!' The little voice shouting in her ear was filled with emotion. 'I wish I could of come before this!'

'The devil you say,' Mary returned. 'Oh Penny, what a sight. The horses are walking backwards and sideways, and all the anti-people are running across the street into the Common. You know about the Common?'

'Nope. What's the other crowd doing?'

Mary pulled them both out into the open again. 'Well, it looks as if the other crowd is being pushed up the hill, over towards the Courthouse Square.

Everybody keeps moving to keep out from under the horse's feet. Sit down here for a minute.'

They both sat on the top step, a pair of small urchins alone in a sea of stone. It seemed almost magical, but the street in front of the State House was empty, and only a few people could be seen disappearing into the distance. Two elderly custodians came out on to the pavement in front of them and began a slow clean up. As she saw it, Mary kept up a relentless barrage of words, trying her best to convey to the little girl the scope of what was happening.

'And the Common?' Penny probed.

'Oh. The Common!' She stopped long enough to take a deep breath. Being a tour guide was perhaps somewhat more than her vocal cords could sustain. 'It's a park,' she continued. 'A great big park, full of grass and trees and—and there's a frog pond up at this end, and down at the other end, down the hill, there are the Public Gardens, and the Swan boats, and things like that. I think it's about forty-five acres, and it belongs in common to all the people, so it's called the Common. It's all that's left of Farmer Braxton's farm, way back in Puritan days, when Boston was an island, and Governor Bradford bought it for his new city.'

The voice from behind them was very authoritative, very bored. 'Ladies, you can't sit here. You can walk, or you can dance, or you can sing, or you can petition. But you can't just sit!'

'Come on, Penny,' she laughed, picking up the tiny hand in hers, 'the voice of the Civil Servants has spoken. Let's go across the street to the frog pond!'

They were both exhausted by four o'clock. So much so that the little girl's feet were stumbling as they made their way down the slight incline that was Joy Street, towards home. There it is again, she told herself. Towards home! What's the matter with me? That stupid phrase keeps coming back into my mind, like a joyous thief in the night.

The day had been one of a kind, and it all felt so— homey. She had struggled for years to earn a teaching certificate—to have the legal right to teach a group of twenty or thirty children. And instead she had wound up with another type of certificate, and only one child to teach. One lovely, loving child. There was no doubt about it, the pair of them had an affinity towards each other. They already felt a closeness, a form of love. And the only fly in the ointment was the child's father. Say it correctly, she lectured herself. The only fly in the ointment is my husband! I wouldn't mind if he were only the child's father. He's my husband! A shiver ran up and down her spine. A touch of fear—a fear of the unknown. The sun was struggling lower towards the western hills of Belmont and Waltham. Very soon now he's bound to make an appearance. With the coming of darkness the devil makes his appearance. Cotton Mather said that. Lord, I suppose it's true?

'What's the matter?' Penny tugged at her hand. 'You're talking to yourself, but you didn't say nothing when we went by Mickey the Squirter!'

'And how did you know that, young lady?'

'I don't know. I just know. I count things. And I remember where things are. I betcha tomorrow I could lead you over the whole route we walked today. Did you know that? And when I get to be ten Daddy's going to get me a dog—a special dog. And the front steps ought to be right here.'

And of course they were. Mary led the child up the stairs and into the house, tired, surprised, amused by the little package of humanity at her side.

'Ah, there you are,' Mrs Hudley met them in the hall. 'You look a sight, Penny Richardson! All your hair in a fluster, and your cheeks all rosy!' And so do you, Mrs Richardson, the housekeeper thought as she watched them. A child of—no, children of innocence. No wonder he married you! 'Will you be going up to change, Mrs Richardson?'

'Oh please,' she pleaded, 'Mary. And yes, I suppose we both should go up and change. What time is dinner?'

'Mr Richardson usually gets home about five-thirty.

He likes to have a drink about six, and the meal will be on the table at six-thirty.'

Mary did a quick count in her mind. From breakfast at seven-thirty to dinner at six-thirty, and then all the cleaning up afterwards? 'That makes terribly long hours for you, Mrs Hudley,' she said. 'It's too much, now that there are three of us. We'll have to do something about that.'

Mrs Hudley smiled broadly as she watched the two of them dance up the stairs, hand in hand, giggling at each other's jokes. Why what a surprise, the housekeeper thought. I've seen her go up those stairs a dozen times, wiggling her bottom at the Mister like some street walker. And all that time I had no idea at all how nice she really is. But then again, she *says* she's never been here before. What do you make of that? The problem was nagging, but not necessarily important. She threw up her hands and went back to the kitchen, still smiling.

Upstairs Mary led the way directly to the big bedroom which the two girls had shared the night before. 'Where do you have your clothes?' she inquired, thinking of the little trundle bed in the dressing room.

'Across the hall,' Penny replied. 'I only stayed in the little room for last night. Daddy thought I might be scared or something, and he wanted me to be close.'

'And were you? Scared, I mean?'

'Nope. I don't scare easy. Do you?'

Mary chuckled at the question. How long had it taken her to make the decision to move her mother? And all the time shaking with doubt. Little Miss Mouse. 'Me? I scare pretty easy, let me tell you. Come on. Show me where your clothes are, and we'll both have a shower.'

'Together?'

'Why not. We're both girls, aren't we?'

'Wow! I never did that before! Hurry up!'

'That's what comes of being an only daughter,' Mary laughed as she led the way to the bathroom. 'What you need is a brother or sister.'

'Yes, I know,' the little girl yelled at her as they both

ducked into the warm spray. 'Daddy and I both agreed. But he said we had to be awful good to you 'cos you knew where to get them!'

Very suddenly Mary realised that it was not just the warm shower that was turning her so blushingly red.

They came back downstairs, hand in hand, just as the big clock on the stairs sounded five o'clock. For some reason Mary felt the itch to kick the imperious monster. 'You could have run faster yesterday, you overgrown—regulator,' she snarled under her breath. The clock, secure in its position in life, merely bonged an extra bong at her.

'Are you talking to the clock?' Penny asked.

'I was just clearing my throat,' Mary lied.

'It's getting old. It bongs too many times. Daddy says it needs an overhaul.'

The big ornate hands quivered a little under the threat, jumped a minute marker, and settled back again phlegmatically as the girls continued down the stairs. 'Mary Richardson,' she whispered. 'Mary Richardson. Mary Richardson.' Repeat after me a hundred times. It would be better to practise the name before she faced him. He would surely not appreciate it if one of his possessions got his name wrong!

She had not really noticed until they were sitting in the study how closely her dress matched Penny's. Loose summer shifts, with shoe-string shoulder straps, the girl's in light yellow, with a sprinkle of embroidered red roses around the hem, her own in deeper gold, without adornment. She had left her hair in its own careless riot, the raven curls tumbling down her back. Penny sat down on the hassock in front of her chair while Mary brushed her golden sheen, and then began to plait it. And that was how he found them.

He stopped in the doorway for a moment, drinking in the scene. The two girls were giggling at each other, Penny with her feet squarely on the floor, her hands clasped in front of her, Mary brooding over the child's head, the very tip of her tongue clamped between pursed lips as she concentrated on the unpractised task.

'Stop wiggling, for goodness sakes,' Mary moaned. 'My fingers are all thumbs tonight.'

'Yes, Mommy,' the child responded, in a mournful tone that brought on the giggles again.

'Well!' he said from the doorway.

'Daddy!' The little girl sprang up from the hassock, ignoring the tug as Mary tried to free her fingers from the plait. 'Daddy! Wait till you hear!' She moved across the open room, not exactly running, but not walking either, and threw herself into her father's arms. He swung her around a couple of times, and held her at his chest.

'Wait until I hear what?' He walked across the floor to Mary. She got up from the chair, overcome with the same mixture of fear and expectation that had frozen her at the breakfast table. What is he going to do? Her mind squirrelled around in its cage, and her cheeks flushed before he got halfway across the room. He dropped the child to the floor and demonstrated just what he intended. He swept Mary up as effortlessly as he had the girl, twirled her around a couple of times, and then, with her feet still of the floor, kissed her in that gentle burning way that he had demonstrated the night previously. She had intended to be shy, to withdraw, to struggle if he should—but her body was not prepared to comply. She hung in his arms for a moment like a huge rag-doll, and then suddenly she was squirming against him, trying to get closer, trying to hold on to the sweetness before it had all spilled out of her cup. When he dropped her on to her feet her knees buckled, and she was forced to grab at his arm to keep herself from falling.

Penny, who had been listening intently, laughed. 'That was pretty good, Daddy,' she said. 'Poor Mary.'

'Yes, it was pretty good,' he returned cheerfully. But Mary could see that his eyes had narrowed, and there was a question mark expressed in the way those thick eyebrows peaked. I'm darned if I'll give him the satisfaction, she told herself angrily. He's got the manners of an arrogant overgrown bear! She stamped her feet deep into the thick pile of the carpet, straightened her back, clasped her hands behind her to still her flexing fingers.

'Mary?' He meant to be insistent, and they were both staring at her now.

'Oh, it was pretty good,' she said, pursing her lips again. 'Not bad. I've had better.' She couldn't be sure about it, but it did seem that there was a glint of sardonic humour in those eyes as he glared at her. Evidently Penny thought so too. The little girl squealed in mock terror, and ran towards the door, her father hot on her heels.

Oh lord, Mary cautioned herself. It was pretty good! What an awesome liar you've come to be. One kiss— just a casual one—and I ought to be in orbit around Jupiter by now. What is this man doing to me? If he ever catches me alone with one of those 'little kisses' I'll be down on my knees begging for the full treatment. Keep away from him! Is it still too late to run?

'Dinner's on the table, Mrs—Mary,' Mrs Hudley announced from the door. 'They're both in there, laughing like a pair of conspirators.'

She joined them cautiously, more than a little upset by her own lack of control. He was sitting at the head of the table, with Penny on his right hand. There were two other places set. One on his left, the other next to Penny. Without waiting for signals she powered her way full speed to the seat next to Penny. His eyes assessed her as she sat down, his hand, as he re-set her chair for her, drifted over one bare shoulder. When he regained his own chair she could see laughter in his eyes. That did more than anything else to restore her courage. He's laughing at me! The rotten—the——

'Try the soup,' he invited. 'It's Mrs Hudley's special.'

She picked up her spoon and sampled the clear soup. It's flavour was excellent, but outside her ken. Penny's soup, she noted, came in a two-handled mug, and the child was sipping away with abandon.

'Won-ton soup,' he told her. 'We have a large Chinese community in Boston, and Mrs Hudley favours

Chinese food.' She started to answer, but by the time she had made up her mind about what to say Penny was launched into a wild discourse on their afternoon's expedition. He listened with alert amusement.

'So, you see, they was all there——'

'Were all there,' he corrected.

'Yes, well, they were all there making all kinds of noises and singing. One was Anti, and other was—Pro?'

'Yes, Pro. That's right. Mary's been teaching you new words, I see.'

'Well, yes. Only there wasn't much time to explain it real good, and besides, you always tell me exactly what things mean, Daddy. They was—were arguing about ERA. What's that mean?'

Mary's spoon clattered into her plate, sprayed a little Chinese flavour on the place mat, and clattered to the floor. She bent over, thankful for an excuse to hide her face. When she came back up his eyes were glued to her, and there was a sardonic smile on his face.

'I *did* say I would always explain, baby,' he said, 'but now we have your mother here to help, so we'll ask her, shall we?'

Mary could feel the furnace-effect as the blood rushed to her face. Not here, she prayed. Not now. Her eyes sent him a silent plea for mercy, and his Mightiness refused it.

'Tell the child about ERA, Mary,' he said quietly.

'I—I don't—don't you think she's a little young?' She was stammering. He smiled back at her, the kind of smile one would expect from the shark which is just about to bite off one of your legs. 'No, no,' he said. 'We must answer every challenge as it arises, if we are to have a happy child!'

Doctor Murchison's *Children's Chatter*, her mind told her as she fumbled for an answer. The best in child psychology. Let no challenge go unanswered. A nice text-book. She had managed an 'A' in that class—topped the class, to be exact. But reading about, and applying—those are two different worlds! She focused her eyes, to find both of them waiting for her expectantly.

'Well—ah—it has to do with a new law that we women want, Penny,' she stuttered. 'We women want to have equal rights with men, and get equal pay. And that's what it means. The Equal Rights Amendment.' And now what do you say? How do you go about telling an eight-year-old girl that she should have equality under the law, that she is as worthwhile as—as her father? But having bitten the bullet, Mary was not about to give up completely. She gathered up a little more courage, avoiding the eyes that were staring at her from the head of the table.

'Men have ruled the world for a long time,' she started out desperately, 'and they've made a terrible mess of it. So now we—some of us—we think it's time for us to have a chance to run things—to be equal to men.' She gained more courage as she gathered speed, so she looked him straight in the eye. 'So we want this law. After all, you and I are as important and as equal as your daddy, aren't we?'

The little girl smiled happily at her. 'You mean I could do what I want, and talk back to Daddy, and like that?'

'Well, perhaps not exactly that,' Mary stammered. 'But when you get older, like me, you could. What do you think?'

'It would be nice,' the little girl chuckled, 'but it would never work. Daddy wouldn't let us.' She took another sip of her soup. And now he was openly laughing at her. Right over the little blonde head, and daring her to do something about it!

She did the best she could. 'Well, what does she know,' she muttered under her breath. 'She's only a child!'

'And you should have seen that policeman, Daddy,' Penny continued happily. 'Mary said he was very big. And we had taken off our shoes and dipping our feet in the water at the Frog Pond, and he said something like you can't do that here, lady, cause there's a law. And

Mommy said, the devil I can't. Where's the sign? And I guess there wasn't no sign, 'cos he just sort of wandered off. Wasn't she brave?'

'In the park, yes,' he laughed softly. 'Do you think she's so very brave here?'

The girl reached out a hand and rested it on Mary's arm. The blonde head turned towards her, as if the child knew more than sight could tell. 'She's very brave, Daddy,' she said. 'She's scared of you, and she won't show it.'

'Is she really?' He leaned forward over the empty dishes of the lovely ham salad. 'Is that true, Mary?'

Change the subject, her mind screamed at her. Change the subject. Anything! 'I think Penny enjoyed the walk,' she said softly. 'Do you mind if we tour the city?'

'You make it sound as if she's never been around,' he replied.

'I didn't—I don't imply any criticism,' she said stiffly. 'I just want to find out the rules. If I *were* really frightened by you, I would probably have fits thinking I might break one of your rules, mightn't I?'

He paused for a moment, eyes locked on hers. Then he broke off the intense contact and sat back in his chair, chuckling. 'Of course,' he said. 'The Diplomat. How is it that Margaret seemed to imply that you——'

'Please!' She held up both hands in appeal. 'Little pitchers——'

'And just what do you mean by that?' he asked.

'She means little pitchers have big ears, and you're not supposed to talk about things like that while I'm here,' the little girl interrupted. 'Come on, Daddy. You're slow as cold molasses tonight!'

'Am I really?' His eyes were not laughing. 'Your mother thinks you've been confined too much to the house, baby,' he said softly. 'Before she came, when was the last time you went out for a walk?'

'I—I don't remember,' the child whimpered. Her cheeks were screwed up as if she wanted to cry. 'I don't remember, Daddy.'

'Oh of course you do,' he insisted. 'We've had a long line of women looking after you, taking you out, things like that. When?'

'It—it was the day they had the fireworks, Daddy. The day you took me to the Esplanade, and the band played, and the——'

'But that was the Fourth of July,' he insisted. 'Almost a year ago.'

'Yes, I know,' the child responded soberly. She slipped out of her seat and made for the door. His face was like a thundercloud. 'You mean none of them took you out walking?' he stormed at her. The little girl stopped in her tracks, but refused to turn around. 'Only Mommy,' she whispered. 'Only Mommy.'

It took Mary two hours to get the child to calm down. In between there had been another bath, a leisurely play time, and a long read. Penny sat in bed and read Mary a story from one of her own books, her fingers gliding across the Braille pages, her story unfolding naturally.

'Why that's wonderful,' Mary complimented. 'I can't read Braille at all. How did you learn?'

'I could of learned at the regular school,' Penny replied. 'But then I had trouble with my leg, too. So Daddy had a man come. A tutor? He still comes in the mornings. But not now. We do like the Public Schools do—we have a twelve week's vacation in the summer. Why was Daddy mad at me?'

'He wasn't mad at you, pet. He was mad at all those women who were supposed to have taken care of you. Now, go to sleep?'

'Mary?'

'Yes, dear?'

'I got this electric microphone between my room and all the others in the house. If I need you, you'll come?'

'Of course I will. Now let's get a little sleep. We'll decide at breakfast where we'll go tomorrow, right?'

'Right!' The little hand came out from under the covers and groped for hers. She held it until the tiny frame was still, the hand relaxed. Then she tucked it back under the light covers and went downstairs.

'I wasn't mad at her,' he said grumpily when she rejoined him in the study a few minutes later. 'I was mad at myself. All this time I thought everything was peaches and cream. And instead—can you imagine that! The poor child is a prisoner in her mind, and on top of that I made her a prisoner in the house! Damn!'

'Don't blame yourself entirely,' she said, trying to comfort him. 'There's no blame in Penny's mind. That girl worships you, don't you know? There's nothing you could do, in her mind, that would be wrong.' She sat back in the overstuffed chair, sipping at the long cold glass of lemonade in her hand. 'She said something to me about her accident. Do I understand that she had some head injury that made her blind?'

'I don't want to talk about the damn accident,' he snarled. His hands were pressuring a thick round glass of brandy. It almost appeared that his tense hands would crush the glass.

'I don't need to know about *your* problem,' she said softly, 'but I do need to know about Penny's problem. Did the accident cause the blindness? Will she ever see again?'

His shoulders drooped as if he had suffered too many defeats in one night. Her heart jumped a beat as she watched him. There was so much she—liked—about him, if only he were not her husband. She felt the wild urge to run across the room and brush that lock of hair back, to enfold him, to——

'We don't know,' he interrupted her thoughts, speaking harshly. 'She could see before the accident, and she can't see now. So I guess generally the accident caused the blindness. But we don't know. I've had her to a dozen doctors, surgeons, specialists. They all say the same thing. There is no apparent reason why Penny can't see. But she can't. They keep talking about tiny breaks in the optic nerve, but they can't find one. And all they can suggest is an exploratory brain operation. And that I just can't submit her to. So there we are. I don't know if she's ever going to see again. But I'm afraid she won't. So don't offer her any wild encouragement.' He gulped down his brandy.

'I—I won't,' she said. The big hall clock was striking nine-thirty, and it had been a long day. She got up slowly and walked over to the couch where this stranger, her husband, was hunched over his glass. 'Goodnight,' she told him. She bent over and kissed his forehead, brushing back the lock of vagrant hair as she did so. He made not a move.

She turned away and slowly walked up the stairs. It wasn't until she reached the first landing that she realised. She had spent an entire day in his house, not giving a thought to her father, her debts, her career, her wandering sister!

'I don't see how that could be,' she told herself under her breath. 'I met him yesterday, and I married him yesterday, and I—oh that's nonsense. That couldn't be!' But as she mused her way into the bedroom, changed into her nightgown, and made her way to the big waiting bed, for some reason not quite clear to her, she offered an added prayer. 'Thank You, Lord,' she recited, 'for letting Margaret miss the wedding.'

CHAPTER FOUR

IT was a horrible way to wake up. Someone seemed to be knocking on the door, and her head moved in an unconscious acknowledgement, and banged hard into the solid surface beneath her. She opened one eye and knew immediately she was in the bathroom. The tiny light over the mirror was still burning. Every muscle in her body ached and complained. She struggled to move herself and her toe bumped into the mouth of the cold water tap. Not only in the bathroom, but in the bath! She shrugged her only blanket closer around her shoulders and began to recall the circumstances.

She had come up to bed early, still not recovered from the frustrations and alarms of the past two days, and with the muscles of her legs complaining from the afternoon walk. Without thinking she had wandered into the bedroom, slipped into one of her granny nightgowns, and climbed into the big bed. There were a couple of thoughts niggling at her mind. One was the mirror over the bed. It was gone. She sighed in satisfaction. The other problem was—she just couldn't remember what it was, and drifted off to sleep and forgetfulness.

Some hours later movement disturbed her. She turned her head towards the bedside table, where the luminous hands of the tiny clock indicated one o'clock. Still puzzled, she returned to her normal sleeping posture, flat on her back, with one leg drawn up so that the sole of that foot rested on the inner thigh of the other. And then the bed shook beneath her. She grabbed desperately for the edge of the mattress, her mind befuddled. It couldn't be an earthquake. Boston was very far from any earthquake zone, although tiny movements had been registered in the past within the city limits. Fighting against her sleep-clogged daze, she shifted on to her left side—and her heart jumped into her throat. On the other side of the bed, almost nose to nose with her, was a man. His eyes were closed, and his breathing rhythm was slow and steady, but as one who had never even shared a bed with her sister, Mary was thunderstruck! How could she have forgotten the man. Her husband. Love, Honour, Cherish. With obligations and rights, among which were sharing a bed with one of his possessions!

Mary knew a great deal about sex—all theoretical. And to find herself face to face with it—sharing a bed with it—was too much for her nerves. She flipped over on her back again, and tried to calm her wildly beating heart. Her body rigid, she gently moved an inch closer to the outer edge of the mattress. He paid no attention. She boldly accumulated another inch of space between them.

But something in her last movement gave the show away. Without actually awakening he rolled on to his side, and his massive left hand and arm came over her stomach, locking her in position. She stopped breathing, panic slowly rising. The huge hand flirted with the generous curve of her hip, then slid upward, until it coursed across the lower slope of her breast. Wide awake now, but crammed with the taste of fear, she squeaked a protest, and rolled herself off the bed on to her knees in the thick carpet. She could see that his eyes were open, smiling—no, laughing—at her. She shuddered. He made a move as if to get up out of the bed. She leaped to her feet and backed against the closed doors of the wardrobe, holding both hands defensively in front of her.

'Well, if you didn't mean it, you shouldn't have come,' he said bleakly.

'I—I—you wouldn't believe—I forgot,' she gasped. 'But I don't—I can't——'

He swung back his blanket and shuffled his feet around on the rug, searching for his slippers. Her mind was turning at three hundred per cent above normal. I have to hide, she screamed at herself. I have to hide.

And there's only one door here with a lock on it! Her hands responded as fast as her mind had. She snatched at the light blanket that lay across the foot of the bed, and ran for the bathroom. She threw the blanket in before her, slammed the door behind her, and flicked the bolt on the lock.

Only then did she realise she was not being chased! Grumpily, completely out of breath, she sat down on the edge of the bath to consider her plight. If he came for her, that tiny bolt would not last long. It was meant to be an assurance of privacy, not a protection against rape! Rape? Surely it would not come to that? She shook her head in disgust. Here I am defending him against my own thoughts, she mused. What to do?

She got up and put her ear to the door. She could hear nothing. If he had gone back to sleep perhaps she could steal out and share Penny's bed? In fact, Penny had twin beds in her room. He certainly would not attack her if she were with Penny. Or would he? As quietly as possible she pulled back the bolt, edged the door open, and peered into the bedroom. All chance of manoeuvre collapsed in her face. He was sitting on the side of the bed, both feet on the floor, smoking a cigarette. She slammed the door and rammed the bolt back in place. She could hear his raucous laughter following her. Twenty minutes later she tried the same manoeuvre, with the same result. She gave up.

The bathroom was small, and the tile floor, even in summer, was cold. The only reasonable space to lie down was in the bath itself. So she wound the blanket around her, turned on the electric heater, and stretched out inside the bath, hoping for the best. It became a miserable night. Not until her tiny wristwatch marked four o'clock in the morning did she actually drift off to sleep. And then someone tapped on the door. And now repeated it.

'Mommy?' Penny's voice, just outside the door. 'Daddy said to come tell you to hurry up. Breakfast is ready.' Wearily she unfurled her bones, acknowledging the complaint from each one. With both feet flat on the floor she stretched three times, did two knee bends, marshalled her face into respectability, and flicked open the lock.

'Mommy?'

'I hate people who are cheerful in the morning,' Mary groaned.

'Daddy said you needed extra time in the bathroom to make yourself beautiful!' Yes, sure, she thought, about a million years worth. If only my bones would stop aching.

'Your father is a smart aleck. When I get my hands on him I'm going to—— I forgot what I'm going to!' She dropped down to her knees so the girl could 'see' her face with those tactile hands.

'You got sleep still in your eyes, and you don't got no make-up on, but you *are* beautiful!' the little girl reported.

'Of course. We're all beautiful, love. It's only a matter of right thinking. Let me find a robe, and we'll go downstairs.'

'Mommy? I called you last night, and you didn't come.'

'You called me?'

'On my intercom. I buzzed. But you didn't come. Daddy came.'

'Well—I——'

'You weren't mad at me?'

'Mad as a wild bull!' The girl's tiny fingers traced a path to the edge of Mary's mouth and found the corners upturned in a smile.

'You're fooling me, aren't you, Mommy!'

'Of course I am. Now, let me get my robe and we'll go down.'

He was sitting in the kitchen when the two girls came down. Freshly shaven, dressed in crisp trousers and open-neck shirt, he looked the very model of a modern major general. The sort of man one could easily come to hate—or love, she told herself under her breath.

'Hmmmm?' he asked.

'Nothing. I was clearing my throat. Is there any coffee?'

'Mommy says she's gonna do something to you cause you're a smart aleck,' the little girl reported.

'I thought she was going to do something to me last night,' he returned, 'but it was all a mistake!'

'Wise guy,' Mary mumbled under her breath as she poured herself a cup of black coffee and sipped its life-sustaining brew. He was staring at her over his daughter's head. Those thick eyebrows flicked up a couple of times interrogatively. She was determined to ignore him. She cuddled her hot coffee mug and turned to the window.

'Penny,' he said, 'I forgot my cigars. Would you bring me a couple from the study?' His daughter smiled acquiescence, and went out of the room, one hand trailing sidewise on each side of her.

'How does she do that?' Mary asked.

'Practice,' he replied. 'Just as long as nobody moves any furniture out of the pattern, she's able to get around the entire house satisfactorily. But I don't need any cigars.'

She swung away from the window and stared at him, a tiny tentative smile working at the corners of her mouth. 'I knew you didn't,' she responded.

'About last night,' he continued. Her eyes opened wide, and he could see the flash of fear in her eyes. 'I'm not trying to force you, Mary,' he said. 'And I don't expect you to have to hide in a bath, for goodness sakes. There are plenty of beds in this house—including mine. You have the right to sleep in any one of them you want to—including mine. But should I find you in my bed, I'll expect that you've finally decided to become my wife. Clear?'

'I—you mean that?'

'I mean it. When you are ready to come to me of your own free will, then come. I won't need any other kind of message.'

'I—you're—very good to me,' she sighed. Almost as if she were not thinking at all she walked across the room, bent over his bright head, and kissed his forehead. 'I do—I do like you,' she said softly. He reached up and patted one of her hands.

'That's fine, Mary,' he said. 'I like you too.'

Penny came back into the room, waving two cigars in her little hand. 'Daddy?' she said. 'What were you two doing?'

'Doing?' he challenged.

'I heard. You were close to each other, and then she moved away.'

'Your mother was kissing me, that's all.'

'Oooooh, that's nice. Can you do it again?'

'Anything for you, baby,' he laughed. He pulled Mary down into his lap and proceeded to kiss her slowly, gently, and very satisfactorily. The little girl came to the table, rested her arms on it, and her head on her arms, facing them both. She gave a little sigh of contentment. 'Is Daddy a good kisser?' she asked.

'The best,' her father answered. 'Mommy can't talk now. She's turning red, and is all out of breath.'

'Ooooh, that's nice. Just like on the radio. Where are we going today, Mommy?' The answer took a great deal of consultation.

He started for the door at eight-thirty sharp. 'Have to catch my regular cab,' he informed them. He walked down the hall with an arm around each.

'Regular cab?' she queried. 'You—we—have a car, don't we?'

'We have one,' he laughed, 'but it's impossible to use in the centre of the city, and there just aren't any parking spaces. Cab is the only answer. We have a regular account, if you need to use one. Get yourself some rest this afternoon.'

'All right.' And then as an after thought, 'Why?'

'Because we're going out on the town tonight. To the Shubert Theater, to see a revival of Noel Coward's *Private Lives*.'

He didn't wait for a yea or a nay from her, but kissed them both rather soundly, and walked off. She sighed after him, watching until the cab disappeared around the corner. I wish, she thought. I wish he wouldn't treat me as if I were Penny's age!

All of which brought the ladies of his establishment to a rather long coffee conference around the kitchen table, where plans for an urban picnic ensued. 'Down at the Public Gardens,' Mrs Hudley informed them both. 'I'll whip you up a couple of sandwiches to carry in your pockets. You can buy drinks almost anywhere down there.'

'There's nobody at the Great and General Court,' Penny complained ten minutes later. 'Don't they got no demonstrations for today?'

'I don't know,' Mary chuckled. 'There are a bunch of people going into the building with signs. I can't tell what the signs say.'

The guard at the door filled in the blanks. 'Budget hearings,' he gruffed at them. 'In the Main Hearing Room. The Welfare Mothers are in the hearing room in force. Something to do with money for the Aid to Dependent Children. Go ahead in, if you're a welfare mother. Or the Chambers are empty until two o'clock. Maybe your little girl would like to sneak in and see the Sacred Cod?'

'No—no thank you,' Mary said. 'Come on, Penny, it's a long walk down to the Public Gardens. They're clear at the bottom end of the Common.'

'But I want to see the Sacred Cod!'

'You can't see the Sacred Cod. It's a carving hanging way up on the wall behind the Speaker's chair.'

'You mean we can't eat it?'

'Course not, silly. You'd get splinters in your mouth.'

'Then what's it for?'

'It's the symbol of the Commonwealth. A long time ago Massachusetts lived by catching the codfish that swam just off-shore. They've all gone now, moved north to Greenland. But the Sacred Cod is still the State symbol. C'mon now—if we dilly dally in the middle of Beacon Street somebody will turn us into a symbol!'

What with one thing or another they dallied their way down to the gardens, walked a while through the floral displays, ate their lunch by the lake, and then took a leisurely ride on a Swanboat. It took a mint of description to paint the picture for Penny, but when people around them noticed what was going on, other voices chipped in, and Mary was able to rest her voice on occasion.

The Swanboats in the Garden are actually flat-bottomed barges lined with open benches. In the rear of each barge is a full-blown replica of a swan, big enough so that an attendant can sit inside it on his bicycle seat, and pedal the machinery that moves the boat's propulsion system. Penny spent minutes 'seeing' the shape of the swan, and then shrilled in glee when the attendant offered her a chance to pedal the boat. After her brief exercise the pair of them took seats in the back, close enough so that the attendant could describe for the little girl each of the garden beauties they were passing.

Although both of them sat through the wonderful ride, they were tired when they found themselves on Arlington Street, looking down the summer-dry expanse of the Commonwealth Mall. Good luck favoured them. An empty cab was zipping up Arlington Street. Mary abandoned her dignity, waved, hooted, jumped, danced, and caught the cabbie's eye. And so they came back to Joy Street tired, but chuckling at their adventures. Penny went off to do her two hours of required Braille reading, while Mary stole a quick shower. She came back downstairs determined to help Mrs Hudley with the house cleaning.

As a result, by dinner time, Mary was worn to the bone, and as usual in such times, unable to control her babbling tongue. Even Penny had difficulty getting a word in edgewise about her trip on the Swanboats, and the Sacred Cod. Dinner was a little early in view of the eight o'clock curtain, and Mr and Mrs Hudley had already taken over supervision of Penny's activities before Mary managed to find her way upstairs to change.

There had been one argument between herself and

Harry already. Feeling very sorry for herself, she went to his bedroom to tell him she could not go. 'I don't have anything to wear,' she moaned.

'Man, if that isn't the classic argument,' he snorted. 'You mean you don't want to go!'

'I—maybe that's true,' she conceded, 'but what I said is true too. I really don't have anything to wear.'

'We'll see about that,' he snapped. He walked over to the sliding doors of her wardrobe and slammed them over. With his head turned back towards her he lectured, 'There's nothing I hate worse than a deliberate untruth. You've got plenty—my lord, you *don't* have anything! Is this all you own?'

'I didn't plan to be the wife of some city mogul, you know,' she said bitterly. 'All I was going to be was a schoolteacher. And an elementary schoolteacher at that!'

'Then why in hell didn't you buy something? You had all day yesterday and all day today, didn't you?'

She ducked her head, trying to conceal the tears.

'Well?' he insisted.

'I—I don't have any money,' she whispered.

'Oh lord!' He whacked his own forehead with his hand. 'Didn't I give you any money? Didn't I set up your bank account?'

She backed away cautiously, wondering what game he was playing now.

'Well, didn't I?'

'No,' she whispered. 'No. I don't want *your* money. I just want——'

'Oh hell!' he snapped. But he came across the room and cradled her gently in his arms, cushioning her face against the ruffles of the white dress shirt he had just donned. She immediately baptised it with tears. He held her close until the spasms of crying had passed, then tilted her chin and looked down at her. 'My fault,' he said softly. 'All my fault. I'll take care of it tomorrow. In the meantime, how about this little black number you have?'

And so she went to the theatre in the *little black dress*

that every girl should have. Hers was of lightweight chiffon, flowing loosely from the hips to just below her knees, with a tight bodice and choker neckline that covered everything, but left her full breasts almost completely and indecently outlined. He laughed when he saw it all zipped up, but there was a gleam in his eyes behind the laughter, and it gave Mary a little pause.

He was very solicitous as he handed her into the cab, and when they were both settled in, he took her hand. 'I want you to know how much I appreciate what you've done for Penny,' he said. She squeezed his hand in reply. 'I don't think I can recall anyone I've known in the last four years to whom my little girl felt an affection, as she does for you!'

Mary settled back in the seat and took a deep breath. Words of praise! A tingle of excitement shot through her, giving her an entirely different view of this man whom she had married. 'She's easy to love,' she told him. 'After all, I *am* her mother now.'

'You really believe that, don't you!'

'Of course I do,' she said in injured innocence.

'And what about me?' he continued. 'Was Penny right?'

'I—I don't understand,' she stammered.

He slid across the seat so that their thighs were touching. 'The other night at dinner. She said you were afraid of me. Is that true?'

'I—yes.' She managed to force the words out. 'But not as much as I was at first. I—I think I could come to like you.'

'You only think you could?'

'I don't make friends very easily,' she said softly. 'Margaret is the outgoing one in my family, not me.'

'Yes, well thank God for small blessings,' he said enigmatically. She wanted to probe further, to really discover what he thought of Margaret, but at that moment the cab squealed out of the traffic lane and pulled up in front of the Shubert.

He had planned well in advance. Their seats were in the third row centre. She settled into the plush padding with a grateful sigh. The last theatre she had attended had been a cinema in Springfield called the Orpheus. There the seats had been designed for very thin male customers. These at the Shubert were of more generous proportions. It was a welcome relief.

The house was full, but for some reason she felt lonely in the middle of the crowd. She moved as close to Harry as the seats would allow, and slipped her hand through the crook of his arm. He patted her fingers comfortingly. 'Nice,' he said, barely audible above the hum of conversation.

She made no attempt to talk. The sleepless night, followed by a full day of physical activity, had finally caught up with her. The warmth, the chatter, the solid bulwark of his arm, were producing a hypnotic effect on her. She was swept up in a maze of dreams, each more pleasant than the one it followed. The conversation dribbled to a stop as the house lights dimmed and flared twice, and then fell entirely dark. The curtain rose.

The woman in front of Mary was wearing a bouffant hair do. Mary leaned her head sidewise for a better view, and suddenly found that she was resting on his shoulder. He made no move to evade her, so she brought her other arm over to complete the encirclement of his arm. And then, for just a second, she closed her eyes.

He was following the curtain opening, and the first few words of the opening scene when he heard the little bubbling noise in her throat. He looked down, to find that all their neighbours were doing the same, looking at his wife, with her dark head cushioned on his shoulder, her mouth half-open, fast asleep, as Elizabeth Taylor and Richard Burton began to weave their magic on stage, not more than thirty feet away.

Her hair had fallen loose, and a segment of it fell across her cheek. He swept it away with a tender finger. Where would I be now if I had married Margaret, he asked himself. Out at some crazy disco party, probably, or in the middle of another of those all-night boozebashes. And look what I've got instead. No doubt about it! Margaret inherited all the McBain brass, this one all the compassion! The kind of girl it would be easy to love. Who are you kidding, buddy, he chortled to himself. *Would be easy to love? Is* easy to love! When he leaned over to kiss her forehead all the couples seated around him smiled, and the elderly gentleman on the aisle seat raised his hands in silent applause.

She slept on, from the opening lines, through the intermission, up to the final curtain. When everyone around her started to applaud she snapped to and looked fearfully around her. Her neck ached, as if she had left it at an unusual angle for some time. There was a sprinkling of face powder on the shoulder of his otherwise immaculate jacket, and both her arms were wound somewhat indecently around his!

Her face turned to fire, noticeable now that the house lights had come up. She struggled to free her arms from his, but found that he was not prepared to let her go. When the audience rose for a standing ovation he dragged her to her feet with him. And then the excitement was over, the crowd partially dispersed, and she felt herself to be all seventeen different kinds of fool!

'Why didn't you wake me up,' she hissed at him.

'For what reason?' he asked.

'I—I feel so embarrassed,' she returned.

'I *did* tell you to get some rest this afternoon,' he reminded her. With most of the crowd gone it was easy for him to guide her to the aisle and up the soft carpet to the exit. They stopped in the foyer. He seemed to know ten thousand people, all of whom crowded around for introductions. Names flew past her ears like individual drops of water amid the flow of Niagara Falls. She pasted on her *I'm delighted* smile, mumbled a few dozen returns, managed to keep her tiny hand from being squeezed to death, and all the time her illogical anger was mounting. *He* knew she had been asleep. And every one of *them* knew she had been asleep, and now he was hanging her out on the line for everyone to poke fun at! Damn the arrogant conceited man! The Bishop was the final disaster.

'I vaguely remember the play, so I had to come for the revival,' the churchman said. 'It's not exactly what the Church would approve of. I'm told that some people slept through it!'

'You have to make allowances for my wife,' Harry said. 'We've only been married a few days, and she doesn't get much sleep nights.'

The Bishop looked down his long skinny nose, a smile twitching at the corners of his mouth. 'The guilty flee when none pursue them,' he laughed. 'I wasn't talking about your wife, I was talking about me!'

And put that in your pipe and smoke it, she yelled soundlessly at him. 'So there!' And she could hardly resist the desire to stick out her tongue at his back. Unfortunately her timing was poor. He had just finished his conversation with the departing group, and turned to catch her at it.

'You have a very coated tongue,' he commented as they followed the others to the outer lobby. 'You be sure to see our family doctor in the near future.' She clung to his arm again, suddenly afraid of being separated from him, and being lost in the confusion of the night. But that certainly ended the conversation for the night.

As she expected, no sooner had he stepped out on to the pavement than an empty cab drew up at the kerb. Remembering her own desperate attempts to stop the cab on Arlington Street, Mary was overwhelmed again. Whatever it was in him that caused it, he was giving her a massive inferiority complex! When they were both safely inside the cab she meant to ask him. What to say? Why is it that cabs and dogs and little children seem to obey your every unstated wish? Why is that? Why is it that when I'm *not* looking at you everything is perfectly normal, but when I look I fall to pieces? Why is that? Why—but before she could formulate the rest of her inquisition the warmth of the cab, the soothing motion, the availability of that strong shoulder, were too much again, and she drifted off. There was a laughing, longing smile on her little-girl face.

She was still sound asleep when the cab arrived in front of the house on Joy Street. He paid the cabbie, bundled her up in his arms, and carried her up the front stairs. Mr Hudley was waiting with the door open.

'Everything okay with Penny?' he asked as he brushed by the older man and started up the stairs.

'Restless,' Mr Hudley reported. 'Woke up twice crying for her Mommy. Mrs H is up there now, sitting with her.'

'Okay,' Harry replied. 'I've got the answer here—at least for Penny's problem. You can lock up, Jake.'

'There's a supper snack in the kitchen.'

'Perhaps later,' Harry chuckled. 'I don't think I could wake this one up with a fair-sized earthquake.'

He carried her gently up the stairs to the third floor, and stretched her out on his bed. For just a moment he stood there, looking down at her. In her sleep she looked to be all of fourteen. Her hair had fallen down completely, swathing her head with its dark outline. There was a tiny smile flickering on her lips. Her mouth was partially open, and as he watched she started a bubbling gurgle, then stopped. He smiled, and began to undress her. The basic black dress came off with a great deal of difficulty. He struggled with it for almost fifteen minutes, inching it along carefully, trying not to disturb her sleep. With the dress out of the way he easily disposed of her shoes, bra and tights, which left her lying there in the soft lamp-light, wearing nothing but her smile and a pair of pink bikini briefs.

Where just a few minutes ago she had looked like virginal fourteen, now, with one arm moved restlessly behind her head, raising her full breasts to prominence, she looked like Mother Eve herself. The dish was too much for him to leave untouched. He dropped to his knees by the bed and gently ran a finger up her delectable body. From her knees it went, across the full swell of her hip, into the deep indentation of her waist, and then slowly up the curve of her breast until it rested, king of the hill, on its rose-brown crest.

She stirred restlessly. He held his breath and snatched his hand away. Her smile returned, broader than before. He shook his head, bewildered by his own responses. Then he leaned over her once more and dropped a featherlight kiss on the peak of her breast. She chuckled so clearly that he snapped his head back. But whatever it was that had caused her response, she was still definitely asleep.

He got up from his knees and went over to the chest of drawers where her things were laid away. There were only four nightgowns in the drawer. Three of them were eminently practical granny nightgowns, full folds of soft cotton, high-necked, reaching down to her ankles. The fourth was one of Margaret's which had been left behind in the house. It was a frill of lace and transparent silk with a deep cleavage, knee length. Naturally it was the one he chose. The one he wanted to see her in.

Putting it on her, for what material there was, proved to be as difficult as taking off her dress had been. But he was becoming more proficient every moment in the handling of those glorious curves and hollows. When it was all accomplished, with many more passages of his hands than were absolutely necessary, he slipped an arm under her knees and picked her up.

Mrs Hudley had heard him somehow. When he came out into the hall with Mary in his arms, she had the door to Penny's room open. She quickly assessed the situation, and went in front of him to whip back the blankets of the second twin bed in the small suite. He stretched his wife out on the bed, kissed the tip of her nose, and pulled a light blanket, regretfully, up to her chin. He went over to Penny's bed, left another kiss on that tiny nose, and went out into the hall. Mrs Hudley followed him.

'She's dead tired,' he whispered, 'but if Penny is restless it will be better for them to be together. My daughter seems to recognise it when Mary's in the room. Isn't that something?'

'Not exactly a miracle,' the older woman said, puncturing his little dream balloon. 'Mrs Mary always wears that lilac and lavender perfume!'

'Oh! Yeah, of course,' he said gruffly. Mrs Hudley went on down the stairs to clean up the kitchen. Harry turned around and went back to his room for another cold shower. 'I seem to be taking a lot of these lately,' he mused as the chill water splashed down on his blond hair. 'Something's got to give around here pretty quickly!'

CHAPTER FIVE

THE last two weeks of June were a gift from the gods. The weather was warm, but not hot. Harry took frequent days away from his job, and spent them with the two girls. Penny's tour of Boston had eaten up all the local spots of interest, and travel became a problem, as they added the Museum of Science, Bunker Hill, the frigate USS Constitution, the Franklin Park Zoo, the Children's Theater, and a fifteen-mile cruise on the Charles River to their visiting list. Of all the attractions, however, Penny loved best the contests and demonstrations at the State House, and meandering through Quincy Market, the city's open-air marketplace.

But it was the evenings that spread whipped cream on Mary's dessert. She and Harry developed a ritual sharing of the task of getting Penny to bed, and when the little girl was asleep they would withdraw to the study, where they would sit close together as he worked on papers, and she on her knitting. It was all as domestic and peaceful as her heart could desire. Often during their time together he would stop his work, look at her carefully, and ruffle her hair. More often there would be a pause in the work, and he would put an arm around her, drawing her close to him, wordlessly. She was beginning to feel—well, not quite a wife, but almost.

She was beginning to work up her courage, too. Even to the point of answering back when he made some snide remark. But with caution. With care. She could never get out of her mind the fact that he was a huge powerful male, who could, without even trying, do her a damage in some casual way, just because he was so big, so powerful. Perhaps it was a hangover from what her mother used to say. But whatever its source, it was always in her mind, and made her tread with a light foot in the presence of her husband. Nevertheless, the mini-battle over Mrs Hudley had been a total victory for her.

It all started after dinner one night, when a crash from the kitchen indicated a major catastrophe. She jumped up from the table and ran for the kitchen, with Harry close behind. The dessert course was scattered all over the kitchen floor.

'I just don't understand what happened,' Mrs Hudley gasped from the chair into which Mary had chivvied her. 'I've never done that before!'

'Hush,' Mary insisted. 'You work too hard. There's too much to do around this house, and if your darn employer can't see that, he's blind!'

'Not *he*,' Harry contributed. 'She. You're the chatelaine of this house. If you can't see when you're overworking the poor woman, you must be blind!'

'It's not funny!' She stamped her foot in anger, and managed to give herself a cramp. She danced around the kitchen in agony, growing more angry every minute. When the muscle in her leg finally relaxed she was ready for blood. She stood fiercely in front of him— 'Under my nose,' she said later—and beat on his chest with her two tiny fists. 'It's slavery, that's what it is. There are three of us now. When it was only one of us—when it was only you, perhaps it might have done. But there are three of us to look after now, and it's a terribly big house! Shame!'

'Do I have to repeat myself?' he sighed.

'I don't really need any help,' Mrs Hudley interjected.

'And she hasn't had a pay raise in three years. Shameful! Three years!'

'What's Mommy mad about?' Penny asked from the doorway.

'The dessert got spilled. You scoot out of here,' he grumbled.

'Boy—little pitchers don't need big ears around here,' the girl laughed. 'Shall I go next door and listen?'

'Shut up!' Mary shrilled at the top of her voice. 'Now just shut up!' Everyone complied. In the silence that followed Mary was astonished. 'What was I going to say?' she asked.

'You were going to beat me up, and give Mrs Hudley a raise, and hire some more help,' he suggested laconically.

'Yes! That's my very idea,' she returned. 'When are you going to?'

He took both her shoulders in hand and gave her a tiny shake. 'Look, Mrs Mary Do-Good,' he laughed. 'I said in the beginning that you're in charge of the house. Do whatever you want to!' He added one more shake that left her dizzy. Her mouth was too dry for speech. She dropped into the chair adjacent to Mrs Hudley, and the two stared at each other.

Very determinedly, Mary stood up again, and caught her breath. 'Yes,' she said. 'That's just what I'll do.' And then there was a pause while she searched his laughing lovable face. 'Won't I?' she asked.

Penny, hiding behind the door, ran into the room and jugged her mother. 'You was great,' she laughed. 'Is that ERA?' To which her father added a pat on the bottom, and a small push towards the dining room. 'Not in *my* house,' he said, but as he went out the door he turned to grin broadly at his wife, and one of his eyelids descended in a blatant wink.

As a result, Mrs Hudley's widowed sister was hired to help with the housecleaning, and Mary worked out a deal where the dinner would be prepared by four o'clock, but not cooked. Mrs Hudley would end her day at that time, Mary and Penny would finish the dinner preparations, and serve. Which may have been hard on his stomach, but it made Mary very happy. There is a need in everyone to be needed, she told herself. And she was beginning to feel needed indeed!

But the trouble with nice times is that they seldom herald the coming of the storm. And one did.

Mary and Penny were late getting out of the house on the tenth day of June. There had been a thing about dusting. Mary hated dust, but hated dusting a tiny bit more. So eventually, when the Lord of the Manor made a comment about his desk, there could be no further putting it off. All four of the ladies dusted. Which made it two o'clock in the afternoon before they sallied forth for their constitutional. The sky was dark, and little dust devils were whipping around in the open dirt area of the Common when they arrived at the top of the hill.

It was not only the tenth day of June, but also the last day of the legislative sitting before the summer holidays. As a result, hundreds of bills had to be acted upon, or were dead until September, and each of the interested lobbying groups were parading and pressuring from outside Chambers, hoping to inspire one last vote for their favourite bill. Nobody was expecting trouble. The demonstration groups were more white-collar than blue. The two mounted policemen were a precautionary measure, nothing more. But when the rains came suddenly, wind-whipped, accompanied by massive thunder crashes, the crowd began to panic. And for once the horses were affected too.

Mary and Penny were already a quarter of the way across Beacon Street, dashing for home, when the panic began. Mary tried valiantly to get the little girl to hurry, but there was only so much space that the eight-year-old legs could cover. With heads down they struggled into the wind and rain, never noticing that one of the police horses was out of control, backing up, jumping nervously, right in their path.

Mary had never been a country girl. All her relatively short life had been spent in the city. So when she blindly cannoned into the horse's flank and looked up at the monstrously high beast confronting her, she lost control. And also lost her grip on Penny's hand. The impact sent her sprawling to the ground, doing little damage. She was stunned to see that Penny, lost in her darkness, had wandered around behind the animal and had frozen in position there, not knowing which way to turn. And the young policeman on the horse, unable to calm or control the animal, did not see the girl at all!

Mary scrambled to her feet and ran at the policeman again, yelling. 'My baby!' she screamed. 'Stop!'

'What the hell do you think I'm trying to do,' the policeman roared back at her. She stumbled over to him, putting one hand on his no-longer glossy boot. 'My baby!' she screamed again. The officer, his hands full with a fractious mount, kicked her hand away. The horse took two more stutter steps backward and reared. The policeman, with one foot out of the stirrup, struggled to stay on.

'Stop your damn horse,' Mary shouted at him again. 'Stop!' She beat futilely on the horse's withers, which did nothing to soothe the beast. 'Get away from us, you damn fool,' the officer cursed. 'Can't you see you're not helping!' He reached down one bare hand to push her off again. It was an unconscious reaction on her part. No amount of pounding would stop the horse. No amount of shouting could get Penny to move. So when his hand came down against her shoulder and shoved, she caught it in both her own hands and bit him as hard as she could.

Now it seemed as if both horse and rider were rearing. The officer, unable to control his animal, blamed most of his troubles now on the crazy woman who was screaming at him. In self-protection he whipped his baton out of its carrier and swung down at Mary. She might have dodged, but at that same moment the horse finally backed into Penny, sending the little girl slipping and sliding across the road, until her head rammed into the stone kerb of the pavement. Mary caught only a horrified glimpse, for just at that moment the swinging baton hit her just below the ear, barely making contact, but enough to send her sprawling into darkness in the middle of the street.

She never knew how long she was unconscious. When she came to she struggled to her feet, to find her arm in the firm grip of a policeman. 'Where's my baby?' she screamed at him.

'Is this the one, Bill?' he called up to the horseman.

'That's the one. She bit me, damn it. Assault and battery. My hand is bleeding like a stuck pig!'

'Where's my baby?' Mary screamed again. 'Penny?

Penny?' The street was crowded with curious spectators, but she could see no sign of Penny anywhere. The thunderstorm had passed, leaving wet streets, and fresh-washed air. 'Penny!' she screamed again. The policeman pulled her not too gently over to a patrol car that had just come up. She fought him every inch of the way, screaming and tearing at him with her fingernails, until his partner in the car came out to help. Between them they managed to handcuff her hands behind her back, and force her into the back seat of the car.

'What have you done with my baby?' she screamed at them. They shrugged their shoulders.

'I didn't see any baby, lady,' the older officer told her. 'Calm down and shut off the water-works. If you had a kid, he's probably wandered home by now. Even a kid could see this is no place to be!'

'If I—if I *had* a kid? Why you rotten officious arrogant overweight monster,' she snarled back at him. 'Of course I had a child. And she'll *never* see how bad things are. She's blind! Stop this car. I want my baby!'

'You don't have to be insulting,' the heavier of the two snapped at her.

She fumbled backwards against the door, without realising that police cars provide no inside door handles which their customers can use for escape. Tired, dispirited, confused, Mary collapsed in a corner of the car and let the tears flow.

Four hours later she was dry-eyed, but no less disturbed. They had taken her to the nearest Precinct headquarters, called a paramedic to check her head, and paid absolutely no attention to her monotonous demands that they find her baby. Sitting at the green steel table in the interrogation room she fumbled and fumed, trying to control her anger, trying to penetrate their indifference.

'Won't you please tell us your name, lady?' the sergeant pleaded for the twentieth time.

'Yes,' she snapped. 'Just as soon as you find my baby. Why won't you believe that I've lost my Penny?'

'Because we get ten—fifteen women a day in here

crying about the baby that they've lost,' he retorted. 'The one they lost ten years ago, or left in the bus station ten hours ago, or beat up at home ten minutes ago. All kinds. Look, I'm not trying to ruin your life, lady. I got a wife and three kids at home myself. Why did you attack the cop?'

'Attack the policeman?' She was stunned by the accusation. 'You mean that man on the horse? He was backing his horse right into my baby. She was standing behind him, and she's blind. She didn't know which way to run! That's why! Did I hurt him?'

'Well, he had to go to the hospital for attention,' the sergeant returned. 'It took three stitches and a tetanus shot.'

'Good!' she returned. 'I wish I could do it again. I want my baby!'

'We don't have your damn baby!' he roared back at her. He might have said more, but at that moment the door opened and a policewoman came in. The sergeant was eager to get out of there. He walked over to the door. 'She thinks we've kidnapped her kid,' he snorted as he walked away.

The policewoman sat down in the same chair that the sergeant had just vacated. Mary felt a little edge of hope.

'My little girl,' she said. 'My little Penny. She was with me. The horse knocked us both down. Now they claim there isn't any such person. Why?'

The policewoman was tired. All the officers she had seen looked tired. But at least this one was a woman. 'If the child was hurt, there would have been an ambulance,' she said soothingly. 'That's a different department. Why don't you let your husband worry about the child. You're in a lot of trouble.'

'My husband!' The words struck Mary like another blow to the head. My husband! The man who is going to honour and cherish me. I could use a little cherishing right now. And I've forgotten all about him. Wait until he hears that I've lost Penny! Oh God, I'd be safer if they would lock me up here for a hundred years. He'll surely kill me! Surely! Her head ached abominably, throbbing and moaning at her until she could hardly stand it.

'Your husband?' the policewoman prompted.

'Don't you know him?' Mary whispered. In her confused state it seemed hardly possible that there would be someone who did not know Harry.

'No, we don't know him, and we don't know you, lady. You had no bag and no identification. Your husband?'

'He'll kill me,' she muttered.

'Not here,' the policewoman assured her. 'Later maybe, but not here. We've got rules about murder in the police station. Well?'

'My name is Mary—Mary Richardson,' she said. Just saying the name brightened her up. It seemed to taste good, that name. Mary Richardson. 'My husband is Harry Richardson. At the Investors International Corporation. Didn't anyone call him?'

'Nobody called him, Mrs Richardson. We had no idea who to call. What does he do at the bank, clerk or something?'

'I guess,' Mary said blankly. 'Or something. He owns the place.'

The policewoman scanned Mary's muddy, rumpled dress, her wild-strewn hair, her make-upless face. 'He owns the place?' she asked sarcastically. 'You want to try again?'

'No,' she shuddered. 'He owns the place. Maybe he won't come.'

'Maybe he won't,' the policewoman sighed. When she went out she closed the door behind her, and Mary heard the heavy lock click closed. What have I done this time, she asked herself. I have lost Penny! He'll never forgive me for that! And I won't ever forgive me either. And then I've got myself arrested. That's another black mark against a banker's wife. He'll never forgive me for that either. And now they're going to call him away from his dinner, or whatever, to come down here and—and he'll never forgive me for *that* either.

Please God, let Penny be all right. Let her be well, and cared for, and loved!

There was an electric clock on the wall, well-worn, with two of its major numbers hanging crookedly down. It was terribly slow, she knew. She had watched it since the policewoman left, hours ago, and it had barely managed to complete one circuit of minutes. But now forty-five minutes had passed, and she could hear a thumping of footsteps, like a parade coming down the bare grey hall outside. More than one—man? More than two. He wouldn't come. But maybe he would send someone? Someone who called him 'sir' and took care of the little unwanted details of his life. Maybe he *should* have married Margaret!

The parade stopped outside her door. She took a deep breath to control her shuddering, and backed against the far wall for protection. They won't allow him to kill me in the jail, wasn't that what the policewoman had said? He wouldn't try to kill her. Not Harry. He would just throw her out of his life, on to a garbage heap, and leave her to live out a miserable existence without him! What a laugh that would be. Find her own way without Harry? How could I? How could I be so afraid of him—and love him so much!

The lock chattered, and the door swung back. And Harry was the first one across the threshold. He stomped into the room, his face clouded in anger. She shrank away from him until he stopped and opened his arms. The floodgates smashed open. She threw herself across the intervening space into the comfort of him. His arms closed gently around her, and she burrowed into his cashmere sweater, muttering inaudibly between the gushing tears.

'It's all right, sweetheart,' he said softly. 'It's all right.' One of his big hands stroked through her close dishevelled hair, and then slipped down to her chin. He tilted it up, using his finger to brush away the tears, and kissed her gently. 'Good lord what a terrible afternoon you've given me, love,' he said. 'I thought you were dead!'

'Oh, Harry,' she cried, 'I've been so stupid—so terribly stupid. I've lost Penny. I don't know where she is, and these—policemen—won't believe me. I feel——'

'You don't have to feel bad about anything,' he interrupted. 'Penny's all accounted for. She always wears one of those MedicAlert discs. The ambulance brought her in to Brigham and Woman's Hospital, and I was called within ten minutes.'

'She's—she's not hurt badly? Oh, Harry, I'll never forgive myself for this. Never!'

'Don't worry,' he calmed her. 'Penny's banged up, but she's going to be okay. The doctor says she has a slight concussion, and will have to stay in the hospital overnight. Or longer if we can't get her calmed down. She's been screaming for hours. She says some monster attacked her in the street and killed her Mommy! We've got to get out of this madhouse.'

Still cradling her in his arms he turned to the group of men who had accompanied him. 'Dr Burton,' he introduced. 'Our family doctor. What happened to your head?'

The doctor was at her side at once, probing, testing. With her head bent to one side, Mary could hardly see what else was going on. 'He hit me with his club,' she stuttered as the doctor's fingers ran over the bruise.

'Not very hard, I would say,' the doctor commented.

'He hit you with a club? Some damn cop? Captain, I want the name and number of that bastard, and you can be sure that we will press charges!'

'The officer has already preferred charges,' the police captain at the rear of the group stated. 'He says your wife assaulted him, and committed battery!'

'What's his name,' Harry grated.

'Hold this bag,' the doctor demanded. Harry took the bag, looked at it in surprise, and passed it on to the man beside him who was busily writing things in a notebook.

'Did you hit the cop?' Harry asked Mary.

'Now this antiseptic may hurt, Mrs Richardson. Please don't move your head.'

'I didn't hit him. I tried to, but I couldn't reach him, so I hit his horse. Ooooooooh!'

'Watch it, John,' her husband snapped at the doctor. 'That's my wife you're treating, not a piece of beef!'

'Harry? Shut up!' the doctor roared. 'Come off the big tycoon bit. So she's your wife. She's still a woman with a cut on her head. Where's my damn bag?'

'How the hell do I know—here it is. Move out of the way. I want to hold her. What's the name of that cop, Captain?'

'First sensible thing you've said all night,' the doctor retorted. 'Don't squeeze her so damn hard. There. You've lost a little hair, Mrs Richardson, and you'll have a whale of a headache tomorrow, but outside of that you look pretty good.'

'I—that's because Harry's here,' she announced primly.

'Well of course,' Dr Burton chuckled. 'Funny, that. He doesn't do a thing for me. Except pay the bills. And this will be a big one, brother Richardson. I need a new car.'

'If you are finished with the medical report?' The elderly grey-haired man was another of the group who had come with Harry.

'I forgot, Mary,' her husband told her. 'This gentleman is from the District Attorney's office. And Captain Melnor you know. He's the Precinct Commander.'

Now that she was safe and secure, and in Harry's arms, she began to feel perverse. She had only been trying to protect her child. And they had the nerve to arrest her! Suddenly she saw very clearly that it was not her fault, and as long as Harry was here she could safely tell them all about it.

'I haven't met the captain,' she snapped. 'Only a sergeant and a policewoman. Did you arrest that policeman yet?'

'His name is Timulty. Officer Timulty,' the captain said. 'Why should I arrest him?'

'Because he ran my daughter down with his damn

horse,' she shouted at him. 'What did he think I was doing? A belly-dance for his entertainment? I yelled at him to stop, but he kept backing that horse, and I couldn't get Penny to run. She didn't know where to go. My daughter's blind.'

'Your daughter is blind?' the captain asked.

'I said that. Don't be as dumb as the rest of them in this madhouse. My daughter is blind. She was standing behind his horse, scared to death, and he kept backing the horse up, trying to hit her. I beat on his horse to get his attention, but he just reached out a hand to knock me away. So I bit him. Hard.'

'I'll say,' the captain returned. 'Three stitches and a tetanus shot!'

'And then he hit me with his club! But I saw him. He backed that horse of his right into Penny, and knocked her down, and then he hit me with his club and knocked *me* down, and that's all I remember. I want that policeman arrested!'

'He wants you arrested,' the captain snapped.

'Break it up,' the district attorney's representative interjected. 'Turn her loose.'

'Damned if I will,' the captain snapped.

'Damned if you won't,' the district attorney returned. 'How in the name of hell do you think I could go into court and prosecute? You know what judge and jury would see. Here we've got this loving mother, and a blind kid. I'd be beat already. Then they hear how your cop knocks the kid down with his horse, and she has to be taken away to the hospital. Add on to that, you arrest the mother and keep her incommunicado for six hours! And then, to top the whole affair, your cop whacked the mother on the head with a truncheon, and she requires medical attention of some kind—which you don't provide! Lord, I'd be laughed out of court in five minutes, and you, Captain, you could find yourself back on a beat giving out parking tickets.'

'Well, perhaps you have a——'

'You're right. I have a point. Mr Richardson?'

'All I want to do is get my wife back. What she may

think of in the next few days, I can't promise. Women's Liberation is a hard movement to beat.'

'Okay,' Captain Melnor sighed. 'I apologise, Mrs Richardson.'

'Me too,' Mary gulped. 'I—I wouldn't have bitten him if I wasn't so mad—and so scared.'

The limousine was waiting for them at the kerb. She looked back at the brownstone station and shook her head. 'Why do police stations look so dingy?' she asked him as he helped her into the back seat. Mr Hudley was driving. He smiled at her and started the motor.

'Because we don't spend enough money on them, for the job they have to do. Tough job, dealing with the public. Especially with you, Mary Margaret. Where in the world did you get all that courage? Would you have bitten the horse, too?'

'I—don't make fun of me,' she pleaded. For all the courage was gone. All the anger had dissipated. He pulled her across the wide seat and squeezed her gently up against his hard frame. She sat contentedly for a moment, and then squirmed to get a little closer. Somehow she found herself turned around, bending backwards across his lap, her feet up on the seat. And then he kissed her. Not a casual salute, but a firm strong touch that brought fire in its wake. She moaned into his sweater, squirming, pressing. Until the ecstasy collided with the pain in her head, and he gently put her away. 'Another time, Mary Margaret,' he promised.

She kept her lips clamped shut, but rampaging through her brain was the desire to shout, 'Soon! Very soon?'

They were travelling faster than she had ever moved in Boston. It took a minute or two to realise that there was a police car leading them. The trip from the police station to the third floor of Brigham and Women's Hospital took thirteen minutes, including the wait in the lobby for the elevator.

Harry held her arm as they walked down the corridor, paying no heed to the flux of official traffic going the other way. But when she heard the sobbing in the distance she broke away from him and ran. Ran to the open door, and into the private room, where Penny, looking tiny in the middle of the big hospital bed, sat weeping her heart out. They were still ten paces apart when the little girl stifled her sobs, and cocked her ear.

'Mama?'

'I'm here, baby!' Mary threw herself across the bed and scooped the little girl up in her arms. 'I'm here, baby,' she murmured into the golden curls. The child sniffled, cleared her throat, and smiled.

'I thought they killed you,' she said. 'There was this monster thing that whacked into me, and then I couldn't feel you near any more, and I was scared—until Daddy came.'

'Me too,' Mary returned. 'Scared half to death!'

'Thank God for Daddy!'

'Yes. Thank God for Daddy. Come on now, settle down. Did you eat your dinner?'

'No. I couldn't eat nothing.'

'It looks nice. Sit back there and let me feed you.'

'I'm not a baby, Mommy. I can feed myself!'

'Yes, I know. But I enjoy doing it. You're not going to be a spoilsport, are you? It looks like chicken soup. Okay?'

'Okay.'

They managed to make their way through a typical hospital dinner, sharing the soup, the tiny chops, and the unflavoured vegetables. When the tray was cleared, Penny lay back into the pillows and sighed. 'I think I need a rest. What's the matter with me, Daddy?'

'The doctor said you bumped your head.'

'Well, I know that. I could have told him that!'

'And then he says you have to stay in the hospital tonight, and when we take you home tomorrow you'll have to be quiet for a few days. He says you have a slight concussion.'

'What's that mean?'

'That means you've got a bump on your head. What else? Now, why don't you lie back and get some rest. I'm going to take your mother home and——'

The child sat upright suddenly. 'No! You're not going to take her away. I want her to stay with me. I want her. If she goes away I won't sleep!'

'But Penny, your mother has a bump on her head too. She needs the rest.'

'There. You see,' the child exclaimed triumphantly. 'If I have to stay in the hospital 'cause I got a bump then Mommy should oughta stay 'cause she's got a bump. And we got this room already, so why can't she stay here with me?'

'Blackmail,' her father snorted. 'Just plain blackmail.'

Mary squeezed his hand and smiled at him. 'I think I want to stay, Harry. She needs more loving than the ordinary girl. And my head does ache something fierce.'

'All right,' he sighed. 'I guess all the world is against me. You wait here. I'll make some arrangement with the hospital.' Making arrangements must have involved some difficulty. It took him fifteen minutes. Mary could hardly stifle her laughter when two husky wardmen came along, pushing another bed. They were followed by the Charge Nurse, who was not happy at all with the change to routine.

'I hope this doesn't get to be a habit,' the nurse sniffed.

'Oh I hope so too,' Mary replied, as meek as she could manage.

'It sets a terrific extra load on the staff, you know.'

'I realise that it must!'

'Is everything going to be okay now?' He was standing in the doorway, but trying to keep out of the way.

'That's my husband,' Mary said, and sat back to await the reaction.

The nurse took one look, and smiled. 'Everything's fine, Mr Richardson,' she chortled.

'I hope it's not going to be any trouble?'

'Not a bit. Not a bit. We have to be flexible in our care for the sick. No trouble at all. Not a bit!'

Mary watched them both, and giggled. She got up from her chair, picked up her borrowed robe, and went into the adjacent bathroom, where she managed to scrub off most of the mud. Her dress was ruined. So were the shoes. But her slip had miraculously survived. She fingered the swollen bruise under her ear, used a borrowed comb to make some measure of order in her hair. I'll use my slip for a nightgown, she told herself, and went back out into the hospital room. Penny appeared to be asleep. Harry was standing idly by the foot of the second bed. The nurse was chattering away at his ear. He looked over the nurse's head, and smiled. She winked an acknowledgement at him.

Mary walked around them, discarded the robe, and climbed in between the cool sheets. Love at first sight, she told herself. They all fall in love with him at first sight. Her eyes were closed when he came around the bed and kissed her gently on the nose. She squirmed under the sheets, and wished it could have been different. This could have been the night when she would have gone to him! The overhead light went out, and the door closed behind the procession of people.

'Mommy?' The voice from the other bed was framed in giggles.

'I thought you were asleep,' she returned.

'Not yet. Pretty soon. They all fall for Daddy, don't they!'

'Yes,' Mary returned. 'Go to sleep, poppet.'

There was another giggle from the adjacent bed. Mary rolled over on her side and pulled the light hospital blanket up around her chin. Out of the mouths of babes, she thought. They all fall for Daddy!

CHAPTER SIX

MARY MARGARET was startled out of her sleep by the morning clatter at six o'clock, as the night team of nurses came through, trying to complete their duties before going off shift. The sun was barely a promise over the distant edge of Logan Airport. And her head felt as if ten thousand devils were at work inside. She grumbled her way into her robe, surprised to find that someone had brought her an overnight bag while she slept. Every move increased the ache. Once robed, she dropped back on to the bed and rested her throbbing head in her hands.

'You don't feel good, Mommy?' The voice startled her. She had almost forgotten where she was, and why. The little girl was sitting up in bed, a puzzled look on her face, as if she too was disoriented. Mary got up and managed to walk around to the head of Penny's bed.

'I think I've got a little headache, baby,' she sighed. 'How do you feel this morning?'

'I feel all right. I got a little headache too, but the nurse gave me a pill for it. Don't you got no pills?'

'No, I don't got no pills, darling, but I'll be all right in a few minutes.' She looked down at the tiny shining face, to where a timid little smile was forming on the heartshaped lips. And could hardly still the jumping of her heart. I almost lost her! And it was all my fault. A tiny bundle of wonderment, full of faith and love and devotion, and I almost lost her! I wonder what Harry *really* thinks about it?

'Mommy?'

'Yes, dear?'

'I want to go home. I don't like it here. People don't feel right. Everything has a funny smell to it. I can hear things that aren't here. You know?'

'Yes, I know, Penny. But your father will be here

88

soon, and the doctor is coming back, and then I think we can go home.' Another nurse bustled in, took Penny's temperature and blood pressure, and started to leave the room. Mary's head was aching too much to be borne.

'Could you get me an aspirin?' she asked. The nurse gave her a curious stare.

'I don't have you on my assignment sheet,' she said. 'I thought there was only one patient in this room.'

'You do have,' Mary returned. 'Only one. My daughter, Penny. I stayed the night with her, and I've got a——'

'I can't dispense medicines without the doctor's orders,' the nurse snapped as she made for the door.

'Not even an aspirin?'

'Not even.' And she bustled out of the room.

'That wasn't very nice,' Penny said. Mary hardly felt like defending the hospital, but made an attempt.

'She has to obey the rules,' she said, trying unsuccessfully to work up a smile. Either the headache was receding, or her other impulses were getting stronger. She was beginning to feel sticky and dirty. 'Maybe if I take a shower,' she thought out loud.

The door swung open on a bulky aide, carrying a breakfast tray. 'Oops, I thought there was only one of you!'

'There is.' Her head was aching too much for further comment. She waved towards the bed, and the woman set the tray down carefully on the side-table, then swung it in over the bed. Mary peered at the food. 'It's dry cereal, Penny,' she said. 'The milk is at three o'clock, the sugar is at nine o'clock. And there's a glass of orange juice at twelve.' Which is *something* I've learned, she told herself. Treat the plate like the face of the clock, with twelve directly opposite the eater, and the remaining directions spelled out clockwise around the circle. Penny's little hand slid around the bowl to confirm things, and then unerringly picked up the spoon.

'I've got it, Mommy,' she said. 'Why don't you go take that shower?'

Mary watched with amazement as the clever hands served as eyes for the little girl. It was just something she had not got accustomed to, this miracle in the darkness. 'I think I will—take a shower, that is.' The aide, who was still watching in some amazement herself, offered to escort Mary down the hall.

'We don't have showers or baths in the little bathrooms with these private rooms,' the aide told her. 'But there's a block of showers along the corridor.'

'And you will be all right, Penny, if I leave you for a few minutes?'

'It's okay. I'm not really afraid. Now that I know you're near I feel a lot better. Take your time.'

Mary snatched up the overnight bag, a towel, and soap, and followed the aide's broad retreating back down the hall. The shower was cool and refreshing, and did a little to alleviate the pain in her pounding head. She managed to dry herself on the small hospital towels, combed her hair over the black and blue mark on her cheek, and wandered back towards Penny's room.

Even with a headache the world seemed ever so much better than yesterday afternoon. All of her *family* were gathered safely around her. What a funny word, family. She had always wanted a family. A real one, where you could joke and play and be serious, where you could love and cherish and be cherished. It hurt to remember all those childhood years when she had vainly tried to be a friend to Margaret, only to be rebuffed by the admitted beauty of the family. And hadn't that resentment been part of the reason why she had packed her mother up and moved away? 'Broke up the family,' is what Harry had said on that first day. And it was true. She had broken up her family—if there was anything there to be broken? Could the McBains have become a happy caring group if she had held her temper and not moved out? It was a question which had haunted her for years, a question for which she still had no answer.

And a pet phrase of her father's still haunted her. 'Margaret is the nice one in our family. If it hadn't been for you prudes we could all have been happy together!' Deep in thought, bothered by the gloom they engendered, Mary felt the brightness fade from the day, leaving her in a world of uniform grey, to match the colour of the hospital's walls. She turned into Penny's room, head down, a twist of pain at the corner of her mouth, and ran smack into Harry.

'We've got to stop meeting like this,' he said in a deep basso profundo. 'My wife is getting suspicious.'

'Oh—how did you know I needed you?' she cried as she threw her arms around his neck and stretched up to kiss his cheek.

'Well, how about that,' he chuckled. But with her head buried deep in his chest, she missed the little stab of pain that reflected in his eyes.

Penny's spoon clattered as she missed the edge of the unfamiliar plate. 'Mommy don't feel good. She's got a headache, and the nurse wouldn't give her no aspirins!'

'Wouldn't give her *any* aspirins,' he automatically corrected. 'And we'll just see about that.' He still had Mary penned in the corner of one of his strong arms, with her nose buried in his ribcage, as he took two steps to the door and leaned out into the hall. 'Nurse?'

The tone of voice, and his overwhelmingly masculine presence stopped the nurse who had been striding down the corridor, stopped her dead in her tracks. It was the same nurse who had refused her earlier, Mary noted, peeping out from her refuge. 'I need two aspirins quickly, please.' The nurse seemed to struggle with her conscience. It wasn't much of a battle.

Within two minutes the nurse was back, the tablets in a plastic cup. Harry accepted them solemnly, like a king taking tribute from the conquered, Mary told herself. She would have protested if her head was not aching so much. She would have put in a word for women's liberation, and—and she knew it was all nonsense, so she stopped thinking. He pulled her over to Penny's bed, still wrapped in the strength of his arm.

'You don't mind if we borrow the rest of your milk, baby?'

'Of course not, Daddy.' Mary had her eyes closed during the exchange. Now she felt a finger pry at her lip. The two pills popped in on to the tip of her tongue, and the cool edge of the milk glass pressed against her. It was either sip or drown. She sipped. The two pills slid ponderously down her dry throat.

'There now, sit down over here and rest your head.' His arm supported her all the way. Her legs were strong enough to do the job, but it just felt good to be able to surrender, to let him support her weight, to let him take the decisions. She slumped against his warmth, and sank back into the chair.

'Are you all right for now?' he asked softly.

'Yes. I don't want to be a baby. Just let me sit for a few minutes—and——'

'You need pampering, Miss Mary, and I'm the only man allowed to provide that. So sit quietly. It will take a few minutes for the pills to take effect.'

She hardly knew what to reply. Nothing in all her formative years had prepared her for this reality. This warmth and concern. She was struggling to state a concept, but could not yet frame it. And as long as his strength was hers to borrow, why struggle? He sat down on the arm of her chair. She could hear the fragile metal creak under his mass. For just a second she opened her eyes and stared up at him, and then closed them again against the pain of the light. He put an arm around her, his fingers toying with the little curl over her ear.

He was looking over at his daughter, who had just finished her breakfast. 'The doctor said we may take you home later this morning. That is, if you'll be good. Would you like that?'

'Love it,' the little girl replied between gulps of orange juice. 'Will you wait here for me?'

'No. The doctor won't be along for his rounds until eight-thirty. And in the meantime, the nurse will want to scrub you up and get you pretty, and things like that.'

'And what will you and Mommy be doing?'

'I'm going to treat your mother to breakfast. I'm the last of the Big Time Spenders, you know. We're going up to the hospital cafeteria. And maybe that will help Mommy. Now that I think of it, she hasn't eaten since yesterday lunch. Mary?'

'Yesterday breakfast,' she muttered. For some reason, just hearing herself say that made her feel sorry for herself. Even though it had been her own fault that she missed yesterday's lunch. A couple of tears formed at the corners of her eyes.

'Hey, none of that.' He bent to bring his head down to her raven hair. Whether it was the comfort of it all, or the rapid reaction of the aspirin, she was beginning to feel better.

'Are you ready?' She opened her eyes and nodded her head.

'It's better,' she said. He helped her up tenderly, and pulled her into his embrace again.

'What are you two doing now?' His pert little daughter appeared to be all eyes and interest.

'I'm kissing your mother,' he responded. 'Do you have to be so nosey?'

'Well, would you of told me if I didn't ask?'

'No—I guess I wouldn't have told you,' he said. 'For some reason I seem to have thought this was strictly between Mary and I.'

'See what I mean, Mommy? He's a nice fellow, but he hasn't a clue about women. You hafta teach him better.'

'Okay, okay,' he chuckled. 'Now can we go for breakfast?'

'Spoilsport!' the little girl told him.

'I'm ready,' Mary sighed.

The cafeteria at the top of the building was almost empty. Those of the staff going home wanted no part of an extra ten minutes over coffee. Those coming on duty had already made do with the styrofoam cups, the instant coffee, and the stale doughnuts. He led her to a table at the far end of the room, up against the plate-glass window that allowed them a view of the city.

'Eggs?' he asked. 'Coffee? Toast?' She nodded her head, grateful that it no longer seemed about to fall off her neck. He patted her hand and went off to the self-service counter to make a selection. She brushed back her hair and looked out over Beantown. The sun was sparkling at her around the edge of the Hancock Tower. One or two seagulls were chancing their lives against the horde of traffic-helicopters which were reporting tie-ups and accidents over the dozen radio stations in town. Her eyes were just beginning to focus. The pain in her head had receded to a tiny memory, curled up in some corner of her mind. When he put the metal tray down on the table, the clatter startled her and snapped her head around.

'Hey,' he said apologetically, 'I didn't mean to startle you, Miss Mary. Try some of this. It's bound to be nutritional, even if it tastes bad.' He slid a paper plate in front of her, loaded with sausages and scrambled eggs. She stared at it, as if it were something imported from another planet. But what he could not know was that she was not seeing the food at all, but rather seeing him. It was almost as if she were seeing double. There was the calm quiet dignity of an important banker, dressed more casually than usual, in razor-sharp grey trousers and a light sport shirt. And then, wavering in and out of focus, was the blond-haired giant, the Viking, with those two sprigs of hair upturned in his eyebrows, giving the mad impression of Satan's nubs. The spark gleaming in his eyes reinforced the image of devil and Viking, and somehow left the Banker out of the running. She ate him up with her eyes as he sat down across the postage-stamp table and poured coffee for both of them. I wonder if it's really true, she mused to herself, that *all* the women he meets fall in love with him? If it is, I have a good excuse—but if that idea is just something I made up to explain me to myself? Lord, what have I come to?'

'Have you come to the sausages yet?' He snapped his

fingers under her nose. 'Miss Mary? Wake up. Eat something!' Her hand moved automatically to the fork, and her mouth began to chew without command from her mind. It was almost as if his orders were running straight into her nervous system, controlling her body directly, without her brain's concurrence. Yet, as the food settled into her empty stomach it created a hunger. She turned to the plate and ravished it.

He went back to the service counter for seconds after watching her swipe up the last bit of flavour from the plate, using her toast as a broom. And not until she had demolished the second plateful did he intervene.

'How's your headache now?'

'It's gone,' she admitted happily. 'It must have been the food. Or the lack of it.'

'More than likely it was all the excitement. You crammed a great deal of turmoil into one day yesterday, young lady. Oh, hi, John. Join us?' The doctor she had seen for only a moment at the police station had come up to the table, a coffee mug in his hand, his white jacket unbuttoned, and a stethoscope jammed carelessly in his pocket.

'Don't mind if I do,' the doctor said wearily. 'It's been a long morning. If we had fewer fools driving we would all get more sleep.'

'A bad accident?'

'You could say that. But——' He paused to sip at the coffee, and made a wry face. 'I don't know why I come up to drink this battery acid,' he complained. 'If I knew someone at the Board of Health I would have the place closed down. Now, about the girl.'

'What?' Mary prodded.

The doctor turned to her and smiled. 'Generally speaking all she's got is a bump on the head. It might bother her for two or three days. I've left a prescription at the Ward desk for painkillers. You'll see the instructions. I don't see any other damage. If there is a concussion, it's very minor. Keep her in bed for a few days—for as long as you can talk her into it, and she'll be okay.'

For the first time Mary discovered that she had been holding her breath. She let it out now in a loud sigh of relief. 'I've been blaming myself all night,' she confessed. 'I still do—but I don't feel as badly about it now. That was a terrible thing for me to do. I couldn't fault you if you were angry with me, Harry.'

The doctor peered across the table at her, then slipped his glasses down off the top of his head to take a closer look. 'Gave you a headache, I suppose? Seems to me I treat more guilty consciences than headaches these days. Well, that's not what I came up to tell you.' The doctor drummed his fingers on the table, as if trying to decide what to say next. 'Harry, if we weren't old friends, I think I would stop right here, but——'

'I knew it,' Mary exclaimed. 'There *is* something wrong. There is!'

'Hey, that's only a but, not a catastrophe!' Harry's hand came across the table and engulfed both of hers. 'Calm down, Miss Mary. You didn't knock Penny down. It was the horse. And he's too dumb to be blamed.'

'You're just saying that because——'

'Because it's true. Hush up. Go ahead, John, drop the other shoe.'

'Maybe I'm just getting old, Harry. But there was just a second there, while I was examining your daughter. Just a flash, you understand. I was running my flashlight around the periphery of her eyes—and for just a tiny instant, I could have sworn that there was a reaction to the light.'

'I—what does that mean?' Despite her admonitions to herself to hold back and control her tongue, Mary just had to know.

'It means? I haven't the slightest idea what it means,' the doctor grumbled. 'I couldn't have said that twenty years ago, when I was an Intern. Interns know everything. It's only when you get older and specialise that you can afford to say that you don't know. I don't. Look, Penny is blind. She became blind after an accident. We don't know why she's blind. And now

she's had another accident. I can't make you any
estimates or any predictions. And if we hadn't been
friends for so long, I would not have said a word. But
what I will say, is keep an eye on her. A close eye. If
Mother Nature is working a miracle, it could be painful
to the child. And that's my sermon for the day. I've got
to get home for a nap before I open the office this
afternoon.'

The two left at the table were quiet for a minute or
more as the doctor ambled across the now filled
cafeteria. 'Do you——' They both started to talk at the
same time. 'Okay, ladies first.'

'Harry—if—if she could see again?' One of his heavy
hands dropped on top of her tiny ones, imprisoning
them against the cold table-top with a strength that was
almost punishment.

'Don't.' There was bitterness in his voice. 'I
thought—for a year after the accident—that something,
some miracle might happen, and she would see again.
But it didn't happen, did it? I've come to accept the fact
that it isn't going to happen. Any other belief could
only lead to heartache, Mary. Forget it. The Age of
Miracles died out in Medieval times.'

She stared up at him, hardly recognising him from
the cynical tone and the sharp words. There was a
furrow across his brow, and a pinched look around
his mouth. How he must have suffered, she told
herself. And still does! If there was only some way I
could make up for the tiniest portion of that pain! If
only there was!

'Come on.' He stood up, almost upsetting the tiny
table as he did so.

'We have to reclaim our little package.' Mary hurried
with the last of her coffee, then scrambled to get out
from under the lip of the table. He simplified the
process by picking the table up by its round formica top
and setting it aside. Her coffee cup rattled mindlessly in
its saucer, then settled down. Just like me, she thought.
Every time he moves my world I rattle around like a
lost soul—until he settles me down again! Almost

unconsciously her hand reached out to his, and they went back to the lift, hand in hand.

Penny was hopping up and down in her wheelchair, so eager was she to see them. And once again, she knew who they were before they spoke. 'Oh you two slowpokes,' she said, exasperated. 'I've been waiting for you for hours and hours. Where have you been?'

'It's only been forty minutes,' the nurse interjected. 'And we needed that time to get you dressed and ready.'

'I couldn't hurry any faster,' her father chuckled. 'I was chasing your mother around in the lift, and it left me out of breath.'

'Well, that's all right then,' Penny returned. 'Did you catch her?'

'Don't be so nosey,' Mary complained. 'You two are enough to make an elephant blush.'

'Is she blushing, Daddy?'

'I don't think so, baby.'

'Kiss her then. That'll make her blush!'

'You think so? What a lovely idea.'

'Leave me alone, both of you!' Mary backed away towards the door. The nurse, grinning broadly, hustled out of her way. 'Pay attention,' Mary said very firmly. 'Our only task is to get Penny home safely. At once!'

'Too bad. The bird has flown,' he announced mournfully.

'Well, you can't expect me to do everything for you,' his daughter laughed. 'After all, I'm only a kid.'

'Yeah kid!' He took the handles of the wheelchair and started out the door. The nurse stopped him at the threshold.

'Union rules,' she told him. '*I* have to wheel her to the lobby.' He laughed and gave way.

'Women!' he said sardonically. 'I'm henpecked.'

'Darned if you are,' Mary whispered in his ear as they followed the wheelchair. 'More like a Sultan with a harem.'

'You're pretty brave in a public corridor, aren't you,' he threatened. But his arm came around her shoulder protectively and he squeezed her as they entered the lift and started down.

They had to wait for a cab, and when it came it was one of the new small cabs. Her headache was gone, the sun was shining, Penny was laughing, and for once Mary was not prepared to comment about his magic control over the city. He handed her in first, set Penny between them, and scrambled in himself. The springs sagged on his side, and Penny was pushed uphill into Mary's side, where she huddled contentedly. He had just never seemed this big, she told herself as she moved as close to the door as she could. And there's the reason, she concluded. He always surrounds himself with big things. Big cars, big rooms, big ideas. She looked at him over Penny's gleaming golden head, and felt a sudden surge of—gratitude? No, not that. Longing! I'm tired, I'm battered, and I want him, she told herself. I just plain want him! Her entire body shivered with the strength of the surprising passion that was running riot through her body. Dear God, how I want him!

'Daddy, Mommy's cold. She's shivering.'

'No—no, baby, not cold. I'm——' and she forgot what she had started to say as his arm slid behind Penny, and around her shoulders. The touch was enough to blow her mind. Just a finger-touch, and a tiny squeeze, to let her know he understood.

'Hey, if you two want to do all that hugging and kissin' stuff, remember I'm in the middle,' Penny squeaked. But there was a very satisfied smile on the little girl's face as they pulled up in front of the house on Joy Street.

It was a smile that faded quickly. The idea of coming home had been like a spur to the child, but after a brief blooming she was tired to the bone, and her headache had returned. Harry bundled her up in his arms and carried her straight upstairs. Mary undressed the child, and tucked her in. Her eyes closed almost immediately, and she dropped off into a fitful sleep. Mary sat at the bedside for a few minutes, admiring the pencil-thin princess who had so touched her heart. Then she turned on the electronic monitor and started downstairs.

Harry met her halfway, on his way up the stairs. 'She's sleeping,' Mary reported. He engulfed her in a bear hug. 'And you need to, also,' he commanded. She snuggled against him with a contented sigh. The shivering madness she had felt in the cab had passed. Now she felt a deep sense of contentment. She *was* tired, she admitted to herself. A night of sleep in a hospital bed was not really a rest. But there were duties. 'I have to check with Mrs Hudley about the supper,' she told him.

'Later, woman.' He swung her up in his arms and retraced her steps into the bedroom. He tucked her into the old Salem rocking chair that sat by the windows while he made her bed ready. When he came over for her, she felt a little twinge of alarm. Which he noticed.

'Not all that brave yet, are we?' He chuckled as he picked her up again. No *we* are not, her mind screamed at her. What is he up to now? He sat down on the bed, holding her close in his lap. His fingers rambled down her legs and flicked off her shoes. Then they wandered back up to her knees. She shivered uncontrollably, squeezing her eyes tight against the broad grin on his face. It was worse, being in the dark, waiting, but she lacked the courage to watch.

His hands marched up over her breasts to the shoestring straps of her light summer dress. They slipped off her shoulders, falling in tiny ripples to her waist. Gently, he set her on her feet. The dress fell to the floor, followed quickly, under his urging, by the tiny pink briefs she had donned that morning. Her chin, which she was determined to hold up, failed the test, and fell, brushing her raven hair forward around her face. She steeled herself for whatever might follow, bringing her heels close together, squaring her shoulders, crossing her arms over her breasts. His hands moved hers away, and her bra fell to join the other discards.

What is he going to do now, her brain queried. Her

body was quivering, her mind confused. A lifetime of training and ethics screamed at her to run. A month of memories hammered at her to submit. This is not a replay of our first night, she told herself sternly. I don't know what he's going to do, but whatever it is, I'm not going to fight him. If he wants me—I—well, I may not co-operate, but I won't fight!

His left arm slid under her knees, and he picked her up, making contact, flesh to flesh. The warmth of his bare arm sent contractions up and down her spine again. If he's going to do it now, I won't be able to stop him, she lectured herself, so I may as well lie back and enjoy it! She felt the faint touch of sweetness, as his lips swept across each of her breasts in turn. She stiffened in his arms—and then, suddenly, he was laughing as he stretched her out on the bed and pulled the sheet up—reluctantly—to cover her. 'And I do mean sleep,' he muttered in her ear as he kissed the tip of her nose and went.

Why that—that—ingrate! She lay perfectly still, flat on her back, with her legs straight and her arms stiff at her sides, as she struggled to regain control of her traitorous body. And that—monstrous man! To—to do nothing! It was ten times worse than if he had done *something*. The thought fed her anger, but it was a weak flame, and flickered out as she smiled at herself, and dropped off to sleep.

Penny woke her up at four o'clock in the afternoon. The little girl was struggling again with a headache. Mary managed to subdue her own weary spirit, found a robe, and hurried over to the other bed. 'What hurts, baby?'

'My head, Mommy. It feels terrible.' Mary brushed back the girl's long hair soothingly while her eyes searched for the little vial of pills. 'Here. Take two of these, love. And some of this water.'

'I—it's hard to swallow such big pills.'

'Get them all the way down. There's a good girl. Now, settle back and you'll feel better quickly.' The girl sighed and lay back against the stack of pillows behind her. Her little face was drawn, the pain furrows deep in her forehead. 'Where does it hurt? On the bump?'

'Nope. The bump is on the back of my head, way back here.' Penny's fingers guided Mary's hand to the swollen area at the back of her head. 'It's not *terrible* bad. It just aches. All up in front here, around my nose, and my eyes, and my forehead. I guess I must be a crybaby, or somethin'. I want——'

'You want what, dear?'

'You'd think I was *really* a baby if I told you.'

'No I won't. What is it that you want? Just tell me.'

'I want you to hold me. Hold me tight? I'm scared of being all alone in the dark!'

'You'll never be alone in the dark again, baby. Not anymore.' Mary eyed the old rocking chair by the window. She snatched up one of the light blankets from the foot of her own bed, wrapped the girl in it, then picked her up and carried her to the chair. When Harry came into the room about an hour later, carrying a supper tray for them both, they were huddled together in the chair, the little golden head nestling just under the cloud of raven curls, both asleep. But Mary's foot was still pushing against the floor, swinging the rocking chair back and forth.

The noise he made brought them both back. 'Oh lord,' Mary sighed. 'My arm is killing me! How do you feel, love?'

The little girl sat up in her lap, smiled, and stretched. 'I feel pretty good,' she admitted. 'Did I put your arm to sleep?'

'No. I think it's fallen off,' Mary chuckled. Harry set out the dishes on the desk between the two beds, then came over and relieved Mary of her burden. She struggled up out of the rocking chair, stamping her foot and swinging her arm to restore circulation. 'What's for supper?'

'*Oeuf sur le plat*,' he announced grandiloquently.

'It looks like fried eggs to me,' she said suspiciously.

'Nobody likes a smart aleck,' he reminded her. 'Eat. You surely didn't expect me to cook a three-course meal, did you? What the devil was that stuff soaking in the pot?'

'Pork chops,' she answered solemnly. 'Braised and barbecued. And I didn't expect you to cook *anything*. I didn't know you could. It looks wonderful. Just what I wanted. Just what you wanted too, Penny, wasn't it?'

'Don't coax the little girl into bad habits,' he snapped at her. 'And that's not all I can cook. I can also hardboil eggs. Do you really like it?'

He had all the eagerness of a young puppy looking for approval. She smiled her appreciation at him as she oriented Penny, and then gulped the food. What a strange man he is! Or were all men like this? He has a dozen different facets, like a well-cut diamond. A complex man, and every new facet added to her love of him. There it is! Her brain shouted at her. That's what's been bothering me all this time! In all his many ways, I love him! How could I have been so stupid as to miss that! I love him! Mary loves Harry! It took a repeated question from Penny to bring her back to reality. She finished off her plate, head bowed to hide the increased colouration of her cheeks. And then she sat quietly devouring him, eating him up for dessert!

That thought was so ridiculous that she dropped her napkin as an excuse to hide her face, to suppress the crazy giggles that flooded up out of nowhere.

'Something wrong?' He leaned down to get a better look at her.

'She's happy,' Penny contributed. 'Can't you feel it? It's in the air all around her. She's dancing in happiness!'

And now I've even got to censor my thoughts, Mary told herself wildly. The child has some of her father in her, without a doubt, but I wonder if her mother came from Salem, the ancient home of the witches?

There was a knock on the door. 'Telephone for the Mister,' Mrs Hudley called around the corner of the door. 'Long distance.'

Harry got up slowly, as if he hated to leave. 'I won't be long,' he promised. Mary walked to the door with him, and collected a butterfly kiss on the cheek for her trouble. Mrs Hudley came in and cleaned up the dishes.

'I could have made something more than eggs,' she grumbled as she piled the plates together on the tray. 'But he said no, he'd rather do it for himself. Some management that is. Hire a cook, and then do all the cooking himself. I hate to have a man in my kitchen!'

She was still grumbling as she went out the door, the dishes rattling precariously on the flat metal tray. Not until she was out the door did Penny and Mary start to laugh. The laughter was cathartic. It started with Mrs Hudley's anguish, and then gathered steam as they both released all the tensions of the last two terrible days.

'And now, Little Miss Muffet,' Mary finally gasped. 'Into the bath with you. We'll scrub you up good and get you a clean nightie, and by that time your father should be back to say goodnight. How's your head?'

Penny slipped out of bed, feeling for her slippers as she came, then stood up. There was a puzzled expression on her face. 'My head is okay. I don't feel full of beans, but it's okay. I just feel sort of— disorganised. Has anything been changed in the room?'

Mary searched the room, knowing how important exact locations were to the blind child. 'Nothing's changed that I can see,' she said. 'Except maybe the rocking chair has been moved slightly. What is it?'

The little girl came over to her, feeling her way cautiously along the edge of the bed, instead of walking confidently as she normally did. When her outstretched hand touched her mother's shoulder, she seemed to breathe a sigh of relief, and pressed against Mary as closely as she could.

'I just have this feeling,' Penny continued. 'Something's—different. I can't seem to remember where things are. Is this the way to the bathroom?'

Mary cushioned the little head against her. It wasn't the right direction. There *was* something wrong. Without saying a word she guided the child in the proper direction. For some reason Penny seemed to have lost her sparkle. She sat listlessly on the bathroom stool while Mary undressed her. She made no objection to the temperature of the bathwater, even though it was a little too cool. She sat in the tub, her mind evidently a million miles away, while Mary knelt at the side and soaped her vigorously. 'We'll leave your hair until tomorrow, baby. I don't want to wash it while that big bump is there. Okay?'

'Yes. That's okay. Mommy? If I ask you a foolish question you wouldn't laugh at me?'

'Of course not. What question could be that foolish? Shoot.'

'Mommy, I——' The little fingers were twining in the golden hair, tugging it into further disorder. There was a speculative look on her face. 'Mommy, that dress you're wearing—it's not a dress, is it?'

Mary glanced down at herself. In the confusion of the afternoon she had grabbed anything available, and had somehow laid her hands on a soft velvet robe, held together by a belt at the waist. And of course the child would have sensed that—would have felt it, just by touch. 'No, dear,' she said quietly. 'I'm wearing a robe, a lovely velvet robe.'

'And it's white!' The little girl's face lit up like a sixty-watt bulb. Mary stood stock-still, in the middle of the bathroom floor. That it was a robe, of course the child could know. Maybe even would know that it was velvet. But to know by feeling that it was white? Not a chance!

'Penny? Did you *see* it? Did you actually *see* it?' Her hands gripped the tiny dripping shoulders. 'Did you *see* it?'

'You're hurting me,' the little girl cried. Mary released the pressure of her fingers at once. There were red marks on the girl's shoulders. 'I'm sorry, baby,' she half cried. 'I'm sorry! I was so excited!'

'Is it white, Mommy?'

'Yes, dear, it's white. How can you tell?'

'I—I don't know. I just know that it's white. I can't see anything, and my head is starting to ache again.' The fire in the girl's face died away, to be replaced by those pain-furrows again. Mary hurried her into a big bath towel, patted her dry, and guided her out to her bed again. Penny accepted the pain pills and swallowed them mechanically. As Mary slipped a fresh nightie over her head she barely moved to get her arms into the sleeves. By the time Mary had settled her back into her bed, the girl's eyes had closed, her breathing had slowed, and she fell asleep. Mary stood at the bedside and stared. The tiny face looked gaunt, tired, but the furrows were fading from her forehead. She looked like a person who had faced a mammoth problem, and conquered it. Leaving herself but a tired husk, in need of sleep's soft hands.

I'm a mother—her mother! The idea flashed across Mary's mind like a newly launched rocket. She bent to kiss the tired little forehead. As she straightened up she felt a twinge in her back, a momento of her own outing. She put both hands on her hips and arched backward, trying to relax the muscles. As she did, she caught her image in the full-length mirror on the bathroom door. Look at me, she told herself. Look at me! In my own home, with my own daughter, and downstairs is my own husband. Lord, how kind you have been to me! She was still musing as she turned on the night-light, switched on the electronic monitor by Penny's bed, and walked out into the hall.

What could it be that was confusing the child? Why had she lost her sense of direction? There was something definitely wrong—or changed. As Penny would say, you could feel it in the air. But what?

She stopped at the head of the stairs, one hand on the banister, deep in thought. Things happen in threes, that was one of her mother's sayings. 'Troubles always come in threes!' What next? A shiver ran down her spine. She shook her head, bringing herself back to the present, but the premonition still hung heavily over her head. She squeezed the little pomegranite knob on the banister, and looked down the stairs. Her husband was standing at the bottom, one foot on the upward tread, his face troubled. He beckoned to her.

She hurried down, barefoot, sliding on the soft silkiness of the rug. The ancient clock on the landing bonged at her as she went by, but she had no time to spare in clock arguments. On the third stair from the bottom she felt driven by demons, and jumped into his widespread arms. He caught her gently, as if she weighed a dozen, rather than one hundred and twenty pounds.

'Penny——' she started to say, but one of his big fingers lay across her lips, enjoining silence. He carried her into the study, and set her down on the couch. At hand on the side table were two balloon glasses. He filled them, handed her one, and took the other for himself.

'I—I don't want to drink,' she protested.

'Drink it.' Almost of their own volition her hands moved, and she could feel the burning sensation as the brandy slid down her throat. 'All of it,' he ordered. Her hand moved again, and it was done. She was gasping for breath as he took the glass out of her hand and set it down on the end table.

'I—I'm going to need that?' she whispered. Her fingers were knitting themselves into a passion.

He leaned over her—loomed over her. 'That telephone call,' he said, 'it was from a man in Washington, in the State Department.'

'I don't know anyone in Washington,' she started to say. He hushed her with a finger. It's the same old reaction, she told herself. I'm scared. I can't stop from babbling. I don't know if I want to know what it is. Maybe I'll be happier not knowing! 'What?'

'They were looking for Margaret,' he said softly. 'For some reason they were under the delusion that I had married Margaret. But my name, and Margaret's were all they had to work with.'

'I don't understand,' she sighed. *I don't want you to tell me. I don't want to know any more!*

'It's about—about your father.' She could feel the tension mount upward in the corridors of her mind, as a thousand devils strained to break through the doors behind which she had long ago locked them.

'It's about my father?' Even to herself her voice sounded stupid. 'They have arrested him?'

'No, not exactly.' He sat down beside her on the couch, and took both her hands in his. He went to Columbia. He took all his money—all his assets, I guess, and went to Columbia.'

'Yes?'

'It's the centre of the drug trade in cocaine.'

'The drug trade? My Daddy and the drug trade? That can't be. What happened?'

'All we know, love, is that against the advice of the American Consul-General in Bogota, he went north into the area which is controlled by the smugglers.'

'And?'

'And they killed him, love. Your father is dead!' He said it softly, and his arms held her tight, but when the words sank in, all the little devils broke loose, and went down the corridors of her mind, screaming voicelessly. For a moment she resisted, but only for a moment. Harry's voice grew distant, echoed, and then she collapsed in his arms, struck down by her own long-buried guilts.

CHAPTER SEVEN

IT had been a long night. As she twisted in her bed, seeking comfort from the disordered sheets, she lectured herself. You really let go that time, Mary Margaret. You really let go. All the heartaches, all the tensions, all the guilt feelings, they all washed out in a flood of tears. The load she had been carrying for years, locked on to her back by her father's wrath, her sister's jibes, and her mother's quiet pained acceptance, all that had come tumbling out for two long hours, under his prodding.

'Your mother wanted to go?' He was probing around the soft edges of the story she had sobbed out to him, until exhaustion had reduced the words to a dribble, a murmur, and she had run down.

'I—I thought so at first,' she sighed, 'but at the very end—she told me that she really still loved him. Can you imagine that? After all the misery he put her through, she still loved him. And in that last twenty-four hours, when I sat by her bed constantly, that's all she could say—how much she loved Big Jim McBain. I know she wasn't always conscious. It was just mutterings. But every word twisted a knife in my gut. When it was over—when she had gone—I sat for three days and just thought.'

'And what did you conclude?'

'I—I concluded that my father must have been right. That I broke up the family for my own selfish reasons. Me.'

She had expected that he would argue with her, but he didn't. Not then. Instead he pulled her close to him on the couch, swung her around so that her head rested in his lap, and coaxed her into putting her feet up. It took a few minutes for her to adjust, to cuddle closer to his warmth. His huge hand rested quietly on her

110

shoulder, while his other hand gently stroked her cheek. 'Cry it all out, Miss Mary,' he said softly.

'I—I have,' she sniffed. 'I've cried out all the tears I have. And on a night when Penny isn't well, either. Oh, Harry, I'm such a fool!'

'No, you've just been under too many pressures. First Penny, then your own injury, and now your father. Relax, love.'

What a lovely sound that has, she told herself. Love. I wonder if he means it? I wonder—how do you really know what men mean?

'Relax,' he repeated. 'Both your arms are stiff. Concentrate on them, one at a time. Tell each one to relax. Keep telling it. Think just about your hands. Tell them to go limp. That's the girl. Now, your right foot. Concentrate on it. Tell it to relax. Keep telling it. And now your left foot. Think just about your left foot. That's the way. Keep them all relaxed. Can you do that?'

She could! It felt almost as if she were floating on a cloud, suspended by a magician six feet above the floor. A wonderful dreamy feeling. 'And now, tell your brain,' he murmured. 'Tell it to shut down. Tell it to receive no more messages from outside. Tell it to relax. Say the word, Mary. *RE-lax. Relax. Relax.*' She tried, and gradually her breathing slowed and steadied, her pulse rate slackened. A vague thought drifted across her empty mind. He's doing it again. Controlling me. And I don't mind in the least. They sat in silence, he gently stroking her hair and repeating a word she did not understand; she gently floating in midstream, adrift from all her anchorages. When he spoke again, it was almost as if he were inside her brain, standing at the controls. His voice was soft, with no hint of emotion.

'When you first left home, did that make your mother happy? Think back that far.'

She puzzled at the answer, until her subconscience sent up the picture of those first few weeks, with her mother happily wheeling herself around their tiny new kitchen, singing as she made the dinner. Keeping herself useful, she had said.

'I think—yes. She was happy.'

'And she didn't become unhappy until she went to the hospital?'

'Not even then. Not until the last day or two, she—she was losing control—drifting slowly away from us.'

'And your sister. Did she come to the hospital, or to your new home to visit?'

'I—No, Margaret never came. I wrote to her twice, and called her several times, but she—you know she led a very busy life?' Somehow she felt she had to get that part in. Somehow she had to make him see that Margaret was—well, Margaret was different.

'Relax,' he said. 'Relax.' She let the threads of her argument fall away from her. After all, he must know all about Margaret, she assured herself. He—they—must have been very close, if they planned to get married, and all. That thought cut at her like another stab wound. No! I can't believe that, she told herself. Relax. I will not think that he and Margaret were close. I *won't* think that. He's mine! And the full impact of that hit her like a sledgehammer. He's mine! I won't share him! Do you hear that Margaret! He's mine!

'Calm down. Relax,' he soothed her. 'Margaret could have come. You know that now, don't you?'

'Yes.'

'And your father? He knew where you were? Did he ever come, or call, or write?'

'I—he—no. He knew where we were. I sent him a registered letter. No, he never came, or wrote, or called—not until——'

'Until what?'

'I sent him a Special Delivery letter when mother went into the hospital. We knew it would be the last time. He sent me a postcard—a picture postcard. He and Margaret were on the beach at Grand Turk island. It was one of those "wish you were here" postcards. Mother died three days later.'

She stirred gently, moving her head enough so she

could see his face. He was staring off into the distance, his expression hardened into a mask of anger, those two nubs in his eyebrows standing straight up in the air. His hand came gently, softly, down on her breast and rested there. 'Don't move, love. Relax. Stay relaxed. Tell yourself again, *Relax*, *Relax*, *Relax*.' She did her best, cutting off all the painful thoughts, until she felt the drifting mode return.

Ten minutes later he snapped his fingers under her nose, bringing her back to the present with a start. 'Do you feel rested?'

'Yes, I really do. What did you do, Harry?'

'Nothing, love. You did it all. It's a form of self-hypnosis. You did it all yourself. Feeling better?'

'Yes. Tired. Exhausted, to tell the truth, but better. Am I explaining that right?'

'Sit up here for a bit.' She was reluctant to leave her warm cocoon, but his arms urged her. She levered herself up and swung her feet back on to the floor. He got up from the couch, and kneeled down in front of her, so that their faces were close together. One of his fingers tilted her chin up slightly, and maintained the warmth of direct contact.

'You've been carrying a heavy load for a lot of years, Miss Mary,' he said softly. 'All needless. Your mother loved you, and you made her last years happy. Your sister, I have reason to know, is completely self-centred. And your father, you must know, was a bent and twisted man. There's no need for you to struggle, love. There's no use for you to feel pain. It wasn't your fault.' And somehow, she believed him. *It wasn't my fault. I tried my best.* But she could not leave it there.

'But he was my father,' she sighed. 'I should have loved him more, and I didn't. I should have. Lots of people loved him. Only me, I didn't. Why is that?'

'Because you knew him too well, love. You were the only one in the crowd who could see that the King was wearing no clothes.' He stood up and pulled her to her feet. 'You were not at fault. Now, I want you to put all that behind you. Your father is dead. All we owe him now is a decent burial. Do you want me to make the arrangements?'

'Yes. Yes, please.' He had lifted a massive burden from her this night, and would do more, she knew. *I'm one of his possessions, and he will always stand up for me. Always!* For the first time that night she managed a smile. 'He would want to be buried with Mother,' she said. 'In Newton. But all his friends—they all live in South Boston. Southie is where his roots were.'

'I understand. I'll take care of it all.' And she knew he would. Both his arms came around her again, and he was about to say something else when the electronic monitoring system coughed at them, and a whimper came through. 'Mommy?'

She broke away from him reluctantly, and stumbled towards the stairs.

'I'll go,' he said. 'You've had enough for one night.'

'She wants me,' Mary said stubbornly. She continued towards the stairs, missing the pain in his eyes, and the murmured,

'Yes she does.'

It felt good to be doing something. To have a goal that could be reached by physical effort. By the time she reached the top of the stairs her adrenalin was flowing, and she felt much better, more sure of herself. The night-light was still on in the bedroom, and she could distinguish the shape of the little girl, sitting up with her knees huddled against her chest. The head came up slowly, as if the mass of hair was a heavy burden.

'Mommy? Where were you?'

'I—I had to be with your daddy, sweet. Does your head hurt again?'

'It does, but only a little. That's not what—I—I'm scared. Something's going on in my head, and I don't understand it. I'm scared!'

'There's no need to be, love. I'm here now. I'll stay with you for the rest of the night. Here, take these pills and a sip of water.' The little girl complied. And then,

'Mommy? I don't feel very big tonight. I—I know it's only for little girls, but could you——'

'Could I what, love?'

'Could you rock me again?'

'Of course I can, sweetheart. Girls are never too big to be rocked.' Her hands were busy wrapping the child in a blanket again, and lifting her off the bed. 'Do you know what Daddy was doing downstairs?' She settled herself into the old rocking chair and cuddled the child close to her.

'No.' The answer was drowsy. The pills and reassurances were already taking effect. 'What was Daddy doing?'

'He was rocking me, baby. And it was very nice.'

'Honest? He was rocking you? Just like this?' There was a very weak giggle in accompaniment.

'Just like this, baby. Even big girls like to be rocked. Would you like me to read you a story?' But her audience had already gone off to that where-ever place where dreams are dispensed. Mary smiled down at her, treasuring the tiny form, using one tired hand to brush the long blonde hair back off her face. For ten minutes or more she rocked, until gradually she fell under the spell herself. She was almost fast asleep when the child stirred restlessly in her arms.

'Mommy?'

'Yes, love?'

'Could you put out the light? It hurts my eyes.'

'Yes, dear, of course.' She leaned far enough over to turn off the little switch of the night-light, plunging the room into darkness. As Mary settled back in the rocker again, the child in her arms gave a sigh of relief—or contentment, perhaps—and was asleep.

In her own half-daze Mary shifted to her left foot to propel the rocker, and idly dreamed over the day. A long eventful day. Starting with her awakening in the hospital, the news about Penny, the sudden realisation on her own part that she was in love with her husband, the news of her father's death. And now this. Please put the light out, it hurts my eyes. The sweet little child. Please put the light out! Put the light out! My God!

She barely managed to command her muscles to

stillness, lest she waken the child again. But her brain, back in full gear, was running madly. Put the light out. What colour is the robe? There was no way in the world that Penny could know about the light—or think that it was bothering her eyes, unless—unless it was, of course! And now her brain allowed her muscles to function. She stood up slowly, carefully, and carried the child back to her own bed. With infinite care she tucked her in, smoothing the golden hair over the pillow.

I have to tell Harry! The thought crashed through her muddled thoughts. I have to go down and tell Harry! But no. She had promised Penny that she would stay with her through the night. And that was a promise she would not break! Where the devil was that microphone? The amplifier was still on, but where was the microphone? She felt silly pawing around in the dark, muttering into the lamp, the doll on the table, the music box. 'Harry? I need you. Come up. Hurry!'

Where the microphone was hidden she never did find out, but she was close enough to it for action to result. He must have run full tilt up the stairs. The thick rugs had muffled the sound of his coming, but he was out of breath when he zoomed into the bedroom, and then was halted by the unusual darkness.

'Miss Mary?'

'Here.' She ghosted up to him and threw her arms around his neck.

'What in the world are we celebrating?' he whispered to her.

'Penny! We're celebrating Penny!' For the first time in her adult life Mary initiated a kiss, pressing her softness against his muscles, coursing her lips across his, and then nibbling at his neck.

'Good intentions, lousy aim,' he muttered as he picked her up clear of the floor and rectified the situation. 'Now, tell me again what we're celebrating?'

'It's Penny. She said——' and Mary stopped long enough to marshal the words exactly. 'She said could you put the light out, Mommy. It hurts my eyes!'

'She saw the light? Unbelievable!'

'She must have, Harry. I'm so excited! And when I put the light out she knew it was gone. Immediately, she knew. Oh, Harry!'

'Oh, Harry is right, love. Or more likely, Oh, Mary! You're the cause of it all. Why are you squeaking at me?'

'Because you're squeezing the insides out of me. I have to breathe, Harry.'

Twenty minutes later he brought up a bottle of champagne, along with a bag of potato crisps, and they sat on the rug, in the light furnished by the hall lamp, celebrating. Until the old clock on the stairs struck fourteen.

'I've got to get that thing fixed,' he sighed.

'And I've got to get to bed,' she returned. 'The morning comes very early for mothers.'

'Want some help?' Even in the dark she could see the sparkle in his eyes. And suddenly, for the first time in her life, she wanted very badly to say yes. But there were too many problems yet unsolved, too many pains threatening just over the horizon. But if he asks me again; 'No. No thanks,' she whispered.

'Ah well,' he returned. 'I have a feeling we're getting closer.'

Do you indeed, she asked herself, as she undressed, slipped into one of her old-fashioned nightgowns, and crawled in among the sheets. Do you indeed, Mr Richardson? How right you may be! But in the darkness of the night it was the face of Big Jim McBain that came to haunt her, to taunt her, and she knew that her troubles were not yet over.

It was in the grey of pre-dawn that she made peace with the tangled sheets, and managed to drop off to sleep. Only to be awakened almost instantly by Penny's whimper. Wearily, Mary struggled out of bed and stumbled over to where the girl lay. It was an effort to put a cheerful tone in her voice.

'Headache again, sweetheart? It's time for your pills anyway.'

'I don't know what to say, Mommy. My head doesn't

really ache. It's just—I feel funny. I tried to go to the bathroom, and I can't seem to locate anything. And now—I just feel—seasick. Isn't that silly?' The tired little voice was trying to make a joke out of what was obviously a terrible problem. Mary bit at her lip. The child is disoriented again. The pills? They were only for pain, the doctor said.

'Maybe you should take a pill anyway,' she compromised. The little girl sighed and sat up in bed, obeying without question as Mary dropped a pill on the tip of her outstretched tongue, and proferred the waterglass. 'We'll be seeing the doctor again this morning, dear. Daddy is going to make the arrangements in a little while. Is the pill down? All right then, lean on me, and we're off to the bathroom, right?'

Penny put a hesitant foot on the floor, and took a couple of steps in the direction of the bath. 'You put the light on again, Mommy. I remember I asked you to put it out.'

This time Mary was fully alert, and cautious. 'You know that the light is on, Penny? Where? Point to it.' She knew of course, that all the electric lights were out, and had been out all night. Almost unerringly Penny turned around and pointed—at the uncurtained windows in the south wall of the room where pre-dawn grey was being speckled with flecks of red and gold as the newly risen sun was reflected from the windows of the building behind them.

'Penny,' she said firmly, not wanting to make a mistake. 'Can you *see* the light? Or do you just feel that it's there?'

'Mama?' The little girl moved towards the windows, a look compounded of awe and fear and astonishment on her facile face. 'Mama! I can *see* the light. Mama! It's not very bright, and it isn't little, like a lamp. It's a great big light area. And I can see shadows. Dark shadows!' She turned herself clockwise to examine the rest of the room. 'Dark shadows! And one of them is moving. Is that you, Mama?' The girl's voice climbed an octave, loaded with excitement. 'Move your hands,

Mommy!' Mary complied. 'It *is* you! It *is* you!' She was bouncing up and down now, a wide grin on her face. 'Isn't that something!' she yelled.

That's something indeed, Mary thought, as she sat in the back of the big car, with Penny in her arms, and Harry behind the wheel. Four years of darkness, and now she could see light and darkness. Thank you, dear Lord! And all the rest of the way she dredged up all the prayers she had learned in her childhood, and repeated them over and over. For Penny, and for herself, and for her father, and—for her husband.

'Well now,' Dr Burton said some hours later. 'We've tested every test we can devise. We didn't know why she was blind in the first place, and we don't really know why she can see now. But she *can* see. Not much, but some. And every hour brings some small improvement. If I had to make a medical statement, I would opt for a pinched optical nerve, which is restoring itself now. So we need to be extra careful for the next few days. Her eye muscles need re-training, and her brain needs practise in accepting signals. Until things are under control, be most careful of bright lights—especially the sun. You'll have to keep telling her about that. My nurse has given her two pairs of special goggles that polarise according to the amount of light received. Make sure she wears them, day and night.'

Mary started to offer some polite thanks, but he was gone into another cubicle, and another patient. 'Well,' Harry said gruffly. The day had taken a heavy toll of him. He was not the usually immaculate man she had come to know, and there was just the slightest hint of tears in his eyes. He reached into his pocket for a cigarette, then thought better of it in the face of all the 'Thank You For Not Smoking' signs that proliferated. 'I really had accepted the idea that she would always be blind,' he said. 'I built everything up in my mind with that belief. And now this—this——' he was fumbling for the correct word as he rubbed at his eyes with a knuckle. She dipped into her purse and offered a tissue.

'Miracle?' she offered.

'Yes, well, I hardly believe in miracles. But now this—damnit—miracle may have given her back her sight, and I'm afraid it will take me some time to readjust. If it is a miracle, Miss Mary.' His arm dropped around her shoulder and pulled her close to him. 'If it is a miracle, it's the miracle of you, Mary Margaret Richardson. You made us both happy in our blindness, and now it looks as if you're leading us both back to the light. Do you understand what I'm saying?'

She didn't understand. Not one tiny bit. But she was not prepared to ask for an explanation. It was enough to feel his warm arms around her. She stretched up on tiptoes and kissed his cheek. 'Believe in miracles,' she whispered. 'They do happen.'

All the way home, all of them sitting in front this time, she kept repeating over and over again to herself, 'believe in miracles. Believe!' Until he interrupted. 'Your mother is talking to herself again,' he commented. And then, 'We'll have a celebration, kids.'

'Mommy ain't no kid,' his daughter returned as she stumbled out of the car. 'It's terrible strange out here. I can't seem to remember where everything is.'

'Hold my hand,' he directed. 'We'll have a celebration brunch. What would you like, Penny?'

'Me? I get to choose?'

'Sure you do. A nice salad. A salmon fillet? Something like that?'

'Yeah, sure. Something like that. I want a peanut butter and jelly sandwich. You too, Daddy.'

'Me too? I hate peanut butter and jelly sandwiches. Mary and I will have——'

'That's not patriotic, Daddy. Everybody in America eats peanut butter and jelly sandwiches. Don't they, Mommy?'

And so they set out the good china and flatware in the dining room, lit the candelabra, and ate peanut butter and jelly sandwiches. But even as he faced his sandwich, the world conspired to rescue him. The telephone rang in the study. He dashed to answer it, and was gone for the remainder of the day.

Penny slept better that night. She went up at eight o'clock, and by nine was fast asleep. Mary sat with her, reading another chapter of *Treasure Island*, with one eye cocked on the hallway. When the little girl dropped off, Mary rocked for a while, then quietly closed the book and came back downstairs. The big clock was striking eleven-thirty before he came in. He was carrying his suitcoat casually in one hand, and his shirt was soaked, even though the weather was fine outside. He moved cautiously until he came abreast of the study door, and saw her sitting at his desk, waiting.

'You didn't get your dinner,' she said quietly. 'Would you like me to fix you something?'

'I could use a bit of something,' he gruffed. 'How about fixing it while I get a quick shower?'

She nodded her head, and watched him as he went slowly up the stairs. He wants me to ask him, she told herself. So I won't. I am learning. So what do I care if he stays out at night until almost midnight. He looks as if he spent the night in a bar-room. Now why did I think that? I never knew anybody who spent a night in a bar-room. Not any—husband—that is.

I wonder, if I'm nice to him, if he'll tell me? So she was especially nice, whipping up a Spanish omelette, some toast, and coffee. But no matter how long she sat across the table from him, chin resting on the palms of her hands, elbows on the table, he offered no explanations. And she, being truly Jim McBain's daughter, stuck out her chin and said not a word. Until he had licked the plate clean, and devoured even the crumbs that feel from the toast. And by that time her tongue had been still too long.

'Penny went right to sleep,' she told him. 'She was tired, but not in pain. She really is disoriented. I have to lead her around everywhere. She played in the bath, and popped off after only ten pages of *Treasure Island*. She didn't want to wear the goggles to bed, so I found the little eye mask that I used to wear in the dormitory.

It's a black silk thing that comes down over the eyes and shuts out the light—and I'm babbling aren't I? You look like a pirate.'

'What?'

'I said—it doesn't matter. Are you going to tell me?'

'Yes of course.' He had draped his suitcoat over a chair when he came in. Now he went to it, fished around in one of the inside pockets, and pulled out a pencil-scratched paper. 'Today is Tuesday,' he announced. 'I look like a pirate?'

'Please,' she said primly.

'Okay. Today is Tuesday. Your father's body will be flown in late Wednesday night. I've arranged for a wake at the Sullivan Funeral Parlor, in South Boston. That will be Thursday afternoon and night. Three hours each. The funeral will be on Friday, at Saint Anselms. He will be buried in the family plot in Newton. Does that sound all right?'

'I—we don't have to hurry him to his grave,' she sighed. 'Before he became a—whatever, he had a lot of friends in Southie. We should have two days for the wake.'

'But somebody from the family will have to be there. That's too much for you to handle. You're not all that well, Miss Mary.'

'I'll be all right on the day,' she maintained stoutly.

He sighed. 'All right. Two days.'

'And there's Margaret,' she continued. 'Did you cable Margaret?'

He looked embarrassed, shuffling a finger through the lock of hair that kept falling down into his eyes. 'Your sister went to England. My people can't seem to find her. I've sent cables to everybody I could possibly think of, but no response. We did track down the man she went over there with, but no results. He says it was all a mistake. He's a happily married man, he says, and knows nothing at all about Margaret.'

'Please——' she clapped a hand across his mouth. 'I don't want to hear that part. She has to come. Send more cables. Please?'

'Of course,' he agreed quietly. 'I'll take care of it. But you must rest, Mary. What time did you get to sleep last night?'

'Oh, I don't know. Pretty late.'

'And Penny was up at five o'clock.'

'Just about. It doesn't matter.'

'It matters, Mary. So this afternoon Penny took a nap. And you?'

'Well—I—Mrs Hudley had the afternoon off, so I—I made the dinner.'

'Damn! And I didn't come.'

'It doesn't matter, Harry. I was glad to do it.'

'You didn't think to prepare sandwiches? It's been a hard day, Mary.'

She clapped her hand over her mouth at that. No, she hadn't even thought about that! Serve him sandwiches in his own home? What sort of wife would do a thing like that! It seemed almost like—like sacrilege. Especially after the peanut butter lunch!

'No,' she mumbled, 'I guess I didn't think of that.'

'And now you'll get to bed,' he ordered. And again, before she had given the matter proper thought, her feet carried her away towards the stairs. But she was not so much in a daze as to miss the playful pat he administered to her bottom as she went by him. Or was it playful, she ask herself as she stopped at the top of the stairs to massage her stinging flank. He had hands like—steamshovels. And no matter how softly he intended the swing, the sheer momentum of it gave somewhat more than a tingle.

She showered and went quietly to bed, only to find herself tossing and turning in the grip of a recurring nightmare, in which her sister Margaret was chasing her down a fog-filled road, yelling at the top of her lungs, 'You broke up the family!' In her dreams she ran and ran, and in the end bumped into a telephone pole, which put out arms to hold her, and whispered in her ear, in Harry's voice, 'No you didn't, Miss Mary. No you didn't.'

Over and over the dream sequence ran, until finally,

instead of a telephone pole, she ran into a tiny rag doll, and Penny's voice was saying, 'Mommy?'

Mary shook her head to clear it. 'In a minute, dear.' She stretched mightily, running her hands up the back of her neck under the heavy fall of her hair. Her gown was soaked, as were the sheets. It had to do with the dream—but the sequence had escaped her, and Penny required help. Regretting the lost moment, she swung her legs up out of the bed and set the day in motion.

'I just never knew that being a mother required so much physical labour,' she grumbled lightly as she helped the little girl get herself together. 'And the pay is terrible. Did you know that?'

'Daddy pays you for being our mother?' The little girl was in a teasing mood as they shared a cool shower. It helped to clear Mary's head. 'I'm not *his* mother,' she laughed. 'Just yours. And no, he doesn't pay me.'

'Well, he pays me for being a daughter,' Penny averred. 'Once a week. Two dollars. It's called a 'lowance. Don't you get no 'lowance?'

'Say, I must really be missing out,' Mary chuckled as she rubbed the little girl dry. 'Two dollars a week, huh? Well, I'll have to find him and——'

Whatever her plan was, it came to nothing. Harry disappeared early, pleading the press of work. Penny, still confined to the house on doctor's orders, was mad to explore, to compare the fading senses of her darkness with the increasing senses of her eyes. So they both rattled up and down stairs, in and out of rooms, used and unused, until the day was past, and both of them were worn to a frazzle.

And this time, when he came home at five for cocktails and dinner, Mary had complied with what she thought were his instructions, and set a plate of cold sandwiches in front of him. From the look on his face she knew she had guessed wrong again, but he did eat. And then went out again.

Penny was restless that night, barely dozing off before the return of one of her 'little headaches, Mommy. Not like before. Just a little one.' But no matter how small they were, they disrupted the entire night, and when Thursday morning came, full of birdsong and sunshine, Mary was bleary-eyed. There was no chance for a nap in the morning. Harry hurried her out for a quick shopping trip, after he had combed her wardrobe for suitable mourning attire. And rather than trust her to follow directions, he came along too, insisting she do something about refurbishing her entire wardrobe.

As a result, when they arrived at the funeral home for the afternoon Wake, Mary was already tired. He sat with her, in the chairs carefully arranged up front, for the family. And it was only his strength, from which she borrowed shamelessly, that kept her going. The room was crowded. All the friends of Big Jim McBain came. All the little people, who remembered him and his father. All the greying men who had played football with him at South Boston High School. All the middle-aged, well-married Irish lasses to whom his name still brought a sparkle of remembrance. They came, passed quickly by the closed coffin, said a few words to Mary, and mingled with the crowd. So many old friends and relatives and friends of relatives came that Mary cried steadily, even forgiving those, the majority of them, in fact, who called her Margaret and asked whatever had happened to her quiet sister.

And at the wake that night the men came. The shirt-sleeved men who worked hard in the daytime, and had shared many a beer at the corner pub with Big Jim, back in the 'good old days'. And Mary became more and more tired, more quiet, depending on the blond giant at her side to sustain her as the crowds ebbed and flowed, until finally a young priest came in to lead the prayers, and the night was over.

She barely made it up the stairs when they came home. Her husband settled all her arguments by carrying her up the stairs, as he had done that first day. But this time there was very little huffing and puffing. She gladly rested her head on his shoulder, and dreamed of the time when she might leave it there forever. Mrs Hudley, who had borne the burden of nursing watch all day reported that the little girl had been restless, missed her mother, and still had a small headache.

It was another restless night. Penny woke up at one o'clock in the morning, stayed up until two, was up again at four o'clock, and barely managed to settle down at sunrise. And Mary was up with her, bone tired, but treasuring the tiny mite committed to her care. She had turned off the electronic system, 'so you can get some sleep, Harry. After all, where would we all be if you couldn't get your rest?' To which he had grumpily agreed, but had insisted, after a long argument over the breakfast table that both the girls go back to bed.

The second day of the Wake was much like the first. The signatures in the guest book multiplied profusely. Harry came in just at the dot of two, and sat with her. But there was a third family chair, which Mary had insisted upon, and she brooded over it through tired eyes as the afternoon passed. But Margaret never came.

'Are you sure you sent for her?' she insisted that night at home. There was a hysterical note in her voice, which he noted. And while he tried to soothe her, he made motions to Mr Hudley, who called the doctor.

Mary slept well that night. Well and heavily. All brought on by the needle that pricked her arm while she was still trying to make Harry produce Margaret—out of thin air, if necessary. 'She wouldn't miss it,' she sobbed at him as he carried her up the stairs. 'She loved him. She was his daughter! Are you sure you——' The rest of the sentence was cut off suddenly as the massive sedative pole-axed her. Her head was drooping over his shoulder as he took her in to the master bedroom, undressed her carefully, and tasted the bitter joy of stuffing her into another nightgown. All this before he left her there alone, and went off to share the second bed in his daughter's room. And that night, as one would expect, Penny slept through the entire night, made not a single sound, and insisted that she was going to the funeral 'for her Mommy's Dad'.

It was raining the day of the funeral. The service was held at Saint Anselms, the parish which had known the rich Jim McBain. But still they came from Southie, filling the old stone church till it bulged. Mary delayed at the house until the last moment, waiting desperately for Margaret to appear. The rest had restored her strength, but not her spirits. She felt listless, worried. Her devils were riding her again. Not about her father. She was convinced—Harry had convinced her—that she had done all a dutiful daughter could do. But about Margaret? It wasn't possible that her sister would knowingly miss the services. And yet she did not come. So, at eleven o'clock, with the rain intermittently fighting against a sea-fog shouldering its way in from Massachusetts Bay, Mary Margaret allowed them to coax her into the waiting limousine, and went off to do that one last duty for the man who had given her life.

The church was dark, the organ sombre, the service long. And then the procession of cars, all with their headlights on, seventy of them, took Jim McBain on his last trip. They buried him beside his wife in the family plot at Sacred Heart cemetery, and as Mary tossed her handful of roses on to the coffin, she said one last prayer for him. He was a war-veteran, and entitled to all the panoply of a military funeral, but had never wanted it. He had loved the pipes. So, when the prayers were over, a Caledonian Piper stood sturdily by the grave in the rain and piped him to his eternal rest with 'Amazing Grace'.

The music, and the place, and all the friends, and Penny and Harry sharing an umbrella with her, all these passed over Mary in a soothing amalgam, and washed her clean of all her guilts, and left her at peace. With all the other mourners gone, she said one more prayer for her father. And then the three of them climbed into the limousine, and drove away under a dark lowering sky. As they passed through the tall iron gates of the cemetery, Mary Margaret Richardson felt the weight lift from her small shoulders, knowing there was nothing more anyone could do for James Michael McBain.

On the way home Penny sat in the middle of the back seat, with one parent on either side. Harry moved close to the child, close enough so that he could put one of his long arms over Penny's shoulder and on to Mary's. The move startled her out of her retrospection. She grasped the long fingers, pulled them down to her mouth, and kissed the palm of his hand.

'The Richardsons have been very good to me.' She winged one of her special smiles in his direction. 'I only wish that—I wish——'

'Margaret?'

'Yes. I wish Margaret could have come. She missed mother's funeral too.'

'And left you to do it all?'

'It wasn't like that,' she pleaded defensively. 'Margaret is different. She said she couldn't come. I accepted that.'

'You've never been jealous of your sister?'

'Jealous? Not since we've both grown up. I've been envious of her, certainly, but not jealous. She was always so—so beautiful. You know, she was always the centre of things, full of fun.'

'And you never were? Beautiful, I mean?'

'No, of course not. You can see that.'

'No, I'm afraid I can't, Mary. You *are* beautiful, and kind, and loving, and compassionate.'

'And a nagger,' Penny interjected. 'Don't overdo it, Daddy, or you'll get all mushy!'

'Okay, I'll quit while I'm ahead,' he laughed.

'Such a crowd of people,' Penny sighed. 'You know, Daddy and me, we are all alone in our family. And you have such a crowd of family, Mommy.'

'They're not all close family,' Mary said. 'I have cousins by the thousands. I think the McBains are related to half the people in South Boston, and three-quarters of the people who live in County Clare. And now you're related to all *my* relatives, dear. That's how it works. Don't you really have anyone on your side of the family?'

'I don't think so. Do I, Daddy?'

'You have a grandmother on your mother's side,' he said, 'but she lives way out in California, and is too old to come to Boston to visit. And maybe a cousin or two that I've forgotten. That's about it. Does it bother you, baby?'

'No, not now,' the girl said. 'When I first started reading in Braille about John and Jane and Spot I felt kinda bad. But not no more. I've got you, and I've got Mommy, and what else could a kid want?'

'A brother or sister?' he suggested diffidently. Mary glared at him.

'I don't know,' Penny reflected. 'Mommy said I needed a brother or a sister once, but then she got all quiet and changed the subject.'

'Did she really? How interesting!' She doubled the strength of her glare, but it hardly seemed to affect him. He grinned, then used two fingers to re-shape his face to a solemn expression. 'Your mother has a sister, baby.'

'Do you, Mommy? Is that the girl you were talking about?'

'Yes, dear. Her name is Margaret, and she and I are twins. How about that?'

'I don't know. Is she pretty? As pretty as you?'

'Prettier than I am, Penny, but she looks very much like me. That's what it means when you say *twins*. We're both the same age, and the same colouring. Sometimes people can't tell us apart.' Harry was staring at her, challenging her—to do what? 'You know,' she continued, 'once I dressed up in Margaret's clothes and took her place, and your Daddy couldn't tell us apart.'

'Oh him,' his daughter shrugged. 'I told you. He don't know beans about women. I bet you couldn't fool me. She's very pretty?'

'Oh yes. Prettier than I am. Very much so.'

'If I have a twin will she look like me?'

Mary gurgled, trying to hide behind her rain-soaked handkerchief. 'I'll let your father answer that one.'

She had caught him off balance, but it was only temporary. She could see the gears clicking in his head. And then he smiled. Holy murder, Mary thought, look at that! What a wonderful change. How could any *me* stand up against that sort of weapon? It's like I'd walk a hundred miles for one of his smiles! And why not. I wonder if he knows what he's doing to me?

'I'm afraid it's not possible for you to have a twin now, Penny,' he said. 'To be a twin you both have to be born on the same day and at the same time. But maybe you could have a little brother. A single, instead of an album, if you get my meaning. I'd like that very much. Would you?'

'I guess so.' Penny was acting very pragmatic about the subject. 'Providing he don't mess with my toys and things.'

'And how about you, Mary?' He had baited the trap and set it so skilfully that she had been smiling through the little conversation, and then suddenly, zap. I've got you, Mary Richardson, hoisted on the tip of my spear. How about you, Mary? She was caught so thoroughly that she laughed at herself. And thought about all the love, the sharing, the help, this man had given her.

'Mommy? Do you think I could have a little brother?'

'I—that would require a lot of thought, Penny,' she said. And then lost her head. 'But—yes, I think you ought to have a little brother.'

There was a very large and self-satisfied smirk on his face as the limousine drew up to the curb just behind the taxicab that stood in front of the house on Joy Street.

CHAPTER EIGHT

Mary was the first to get out, puzzling about the taxi parked in front of them, and then remembered to reach a hand in to guide Penny. The little girl was talking ten miles to the minute as she fumbled to get her feet down, but it was more and more evident that that sixth sense which had been her guide during her years of darkness was fast deserting her. She kept her hand in Mary's, and was gently guided to the stairs. Harry came around from the other side of the car and followed them. A burly man, unshaven, with a taxi medallion pinned to his cap, sat on the stairs.

'You the owner of the house?' the driver asked. 'They told me inside the owner would pay.'

'Pay what?' Harry asked, but was already reaching into his pocket for his wallet. 'What is it I'm paying for?'

'The trip here from the Sheraton. There's an extra charge for so much luggage.'

'Mary, you and Penny go inside,' Harry directed. 'I'll sort this out, and be right with you. And you put those goggles back on, young lady!'

The two women walked up the stairs slowly, hampered because Penny kept twisting around to look back down the stairs.

'Do you see something, baby?'

'No. Just some light. Nothing else. Without the goggles I could see something.' The child sounded wistful.

'Never mind for now,' Mary assured her. 'The doctor said it would be a gradual improvement—just a little at a time. Don't be disappointed that it doesn't all happen at once.' She squeezed the little hand in hers. But if it were me, she thought, and I had to wait to see what the light might bring, I'd be screaming blue murder! She's a

130

brave thing, my daughter. Like her father. I hope—I only hope I can live up to their expectations!

'Thank you, Penny, for coming with me this morning. It was a wonderful thing to do. It made me feel much better. Wait while I open the door.' She tucked the girl's hand under the crook of her right arm, and reached for the door knob with her left. Before she could get a good grip, the door swung open in front of her, and the pair of them were able to duck in out of the light drizzle.

'Daddy said that's what families do for each other, so I decided to go. What's the matter?'

The matter was in front of her eyes, but the child could not see it. Mrs Hudley, having opened the door to them, had stepped aside, her mouth quivering. And stacked up helter-skelter in the hall were six suitcases and a trunk, dumped without consideration for order.

'Mr Hudley isn't here, Miss Mary, and she came in, and the taxi driver brought all the—all that stuff in, and she—I just didn't know what to say! I thought it was you, come home early, and I just didn't understand what was going on, because you must have changed your dress, and that didn't seem possible. So I asked, and she snapped at me. Ordered tea in the dining room, she did. And I still thought it was you, until she stalked off and then I saw some of the luggage tags, and——'

'What is it?' Penny wailed, upset by the mystery, and shifting her weight impatiently from one foot to the other.

'It's a lady come who looks just like Miss Mary, love, and that's why I was so surprised. Just like Miss Mary! She's in the dining room!'

'Oh lord!' Mary could hardly contain herself. 'Hold Penny's hand, Mrs Hudley. She is getting lost these days. And bring the tea. Penny, you stay with Mrs Hudley, and come in when she brings the tray.' Without waiting for acknowledgement, Mary skinned out of her raincoat, flipped off both her shoes and her lightweight plastic overshoes, and ran for the dining room.

She was so excited that she flung back both doors

and let them bang against the stops, while she ran into the room. The figure at the other end of the long polished table got up impatiently, and waited. Mary sped across the room as fast as her feet would carry her, and opened her arms.

'Margaret!' she squealed happily. 'You *did* come. You finally came. I knew you would!' She enveloped her twin, nestled her chin on her sister's shoulder, and began to cry. 'Harry said you might not come, but I knew you would. Oh, Margaret!' She was so happy that she shivered.

But it took only a minute to recognise that there was no return to her welcome. Her sister stood in her embrace coldly, making no attempt at all at a welcome. Cold—and sinister—and bleakly bitter. As she felt the cold, Mary's arms dropped to her sides, and she stepped back.

'Margaret?' Her sister was dressed in the latest fashion, a designer dress in flashing amber. The dress appeared warm. Margaret was definitely not. 'Margaret? Papa's dead. We buried him today.'

'I know,' her sister said flatly. 'I got your cables. Or was that some of Harry's doing?'

'I—Harry did it, of course. He does everything for us.'

'Everything? That must be nice for you, Mary. Considering that he's *my* husband, and you stole him from me.'

'I—it wasn't just that way,' Mary stammered. 'You ran off and Daddy said that I—that he——' Her sister laughed and dropped into the chair at the head of the table.

'Don't stammer, Mary. It's all over. I've come back to reclaim him, and you can be on your way to wherever it was you were going. Is that kid of his still living here?'

'Penny? Of course she's here. She lives here. This is our home. We—Margaret, you gave him up!' There was a tremor in the pit of Mary's stomach, a pain that she could not stifle. Because what had been said was all true. She *had* stolen Margaret's husband-to-be. And had no intention of giving him back! All through her years with Margaret, she remembered, her sister got what she wanted. But not this time! Not Harry! If he wants to keep me, I want to stay.

'That kid is why I ducked out,' Margaret said. 'I only saw her once, from a distance, but my hackles went up right away. She's not a normal kid. I know that. Is she retarded or something?'

'No, she's not retarded,' Mary snapped. 'She's a wonderful little girl who just happens to be blind.'

'Blind! My God! Maybe I've had a lucky escape. I need to think about this.' Margaret slumped back in the chair and brought out a cigarette from her purse. At the same time Mrs Hudley came into the room, carrying a tea tray. Penny came with her, clutching at the old woman's skirts. The little girl was frightened.

I've got to get Penny out of here, she told herself. This isn't what I expected! I thought all this would bring us together. Instead, she acts as if Papa and the wedding and everything were all *my* fault. It isn't fair! But something must be done, and at once. 'Why don't you drink your tea, Margaret, while I make some arrangement for putting you up.'

'You do that,' her sister said bleakly. 'And tell Harry I want to see him.'

The words rang in Mary's ears as she marched herself back out of the room, plucking Penny loose from the housekeeper's skirt as she went by.

'I don't like her,' Penny whimpered. 'She's mean! I can feel it all over the room. Is that your sister?'

'Yes, that's your Aunt Margaret.' Mary manoeuvred them both across the cluttered hall to the stairs, where they both sat down on the bottom step. Mr Hudley had finally returned, and Mrs Gibson, the new help, was waiting for her too. 'We'll put her in the Bronze room on the second floor,' Mary finally decided. Her troops formed up, and began moving the luggage up the stairs. Mary sat there as the workers went at it, her elbows on her knees, her chin cupped in her hand. Penny squeezed close in beside her. Harry came in through the front door, tucking his wallet into his pocket. He took one look at the gloomy duo, and sat down beside them, blocking the stair.

'I had to pay the damn cab driver,' he said. 'What's the matter?'

'It's Margaret,' Mary sighed. 'And she's not happy. This time she wants something that I—just can't give her.'

'Oh? Well, we expected it would happen sometime. And you did want her to come to the funeral, remember?'

'How could I forget? I feel like little Miss Muffet, and it's Spider time.'

'Hmmm? I'm not much on nursery rhymes.'

'You know the one. She sat on a tuffet, eating, and a spider came an——'

'Ah. I get it. And frightened Miss Muffet away. Where's Miss Spider?'

'She's my sister,' Mary hissed at him. 'She's in the dining room, having tea, no less. Three weeks of living in England, and now she has to have her tea! I'll go in after a bit. After I get over being sick to my stomach.'

'You know something, Mrs Richardson?'

'No. What?' That did help somewhat. Mrs Richardson. At least he wasn't going to disown her the moment Margaret appeared!

'Life doesn't really have one big crisis, sweetheart. It's a series of little ones. And you must never confuse the two. You're almost the perfect wife for me.' She leaned against him to draw a little strength and courage.

'There's a *but*—isn't there,' she asked softly.

'Your biggest problem, Miss Mary, is that you've got a massive inferiority complex. You are my wife, the mother of our daughter. I will protect you from all the world, but I can't protect you from your own family. You have to do that for yourself. I want a partner in my marriage, love, not some doormat who can be dominated at a snap of the fingers. Now, you have to decide what *you* want, and then do something about it.'

'Okay,' she whispered. 'I'll try. But I—Penny's upset about something.'

'It's your sister,' the little girl interrupted. 'You said she was beautiful, but she's not. She's ugly, ugly, ugly!'

'That's enough of that, baby,' he said softly. 'You don't talk about your aunt like that. Mary, I'll take Penny upstairs and get her settled. You go back in there and keep your sister amused until I come back down.'

'Yes,' she returned automatically, and stood up, brushing down her skirt slowly. 'Before you go, Harry? Would you—kiss me for courage?'

He seemed agreeable, and Penny laughed with gleeful anticipation. Mary had expected something on the order of the kisses her mother gave for comfort— 'Mommy will kiss it and make it better, love.' What she got was a startling spark, an explosion that shook her down to her toes as her lips parted under pressure, and his tongue played havoc with her nerves. When he set her down she was blush-red and panting, and Penny was applauding. 'Want another?' he asked casually.

'That's enough,' she gasped. 'I—that's enough!'

He turned her around and aimed her for the dining-room door. 'Come back with your shield, or on it,' he intoned pompously.

'Yeah. Sure,' she muttered. She ducked under his arm and strode purposefully towards the dining room, but not quickly enough to dodge the playful pat he administered as she wiggled by him.

She stopped inside the door, this time. As usual, there was a shock as she looked at her identical twin. Margaret had her hair up in a modified Pompadour; Mary's long hair was braided, and pinned up in a coronet. Margaret's dress was amber silk; Mary's was mourning black. Except for these two items, the women were now mirror-images. But only on the outside, Mary told herself firmly.

'Margaret?' She hardly knew where to begin, how to

start. How do you patch up a quarrel of years' standing? Especially when everyone—except Harry—assure you that *you* were the cause of the quarrel.

'Mary? No clashing cymbals? No fatted calf? No "glad you could come"?'

'I don't know what to say, Margaret. I'm sorry that you came too late for the funeral. He would have wanted you there. Was the tea satisfactory? We don't ordinarily drink tea in our house.'

'In *our* house? Oh how mighty we've become!' Margaret took out another cigarette and lit up, looking around the room as she did so. 'A gloomy dump, my dear.'

Mary's temper flared. 'It's our home,' she snapped.

Her sister flicked ash on the carpet and laughed, showing her tiny sharp teeth. 'But only for a little while, love,' she returned. 'After all, you married *my* man. You were a stand-in for me, weren't you? And saw your chance to grab with both hands. Didn't like being a schoolteacher, I take it?'

Mary could feel tears welling up at the corners of her eyes, but was unwilling to give in to them. She had too much at stake. 'You could have had him if you had the guts to stay,' she replied.

'Oh my, listen to that. The little kitten has developed claws! Well, I fully intended to marry him. But then Fernando came along. After all, a rich Portuguese Duke is a step better than a less-rich Yankee banker. And besides, there's that child. And now that I know the kid is crippled, well—A pretty kid of course, pretty but peculiar.'

'There's nothing peculiar about Penny,' Mary said stoutly. 'She's a wonderful daughter, who just happens to be blind!' The whole conversation was beginning to leave a bad taste in Mary's mouth. All her life she had believed firmly in 'live and let live'. Only the utmost provocation had driven her to take her mother away from the family. And now that same urge was building up in her, a need to strike out and hurt this cold carbon copy of herself. 'I take it your Duke didn't come up to scratch?'

'Naughty, naughty, Mary. Don't be abusive. But no, now that you mention it, he didn't. It appeared, when we got to England, that dear Fernando had forgotten to tell me he already had a wife. And that she had all the money in the family! It was slightly embarrassing. A very common sort of person, she was, and very brutal about things. When she cracked the whip Fernando bowed out and went home.'

'So why did you come here?' Mary probed. 'Surely after jilting Harry at the altar you can't expect him to have much interest in you?'

'Oh but I do, darling. I really do. It was me he wanted, and unless you're careful, it will be me he gets. All I have to do is snap my fingers, and you'll be finished here, Miss Prim. It shouldn't be too difficult getting your marriage annulled.'

Mary gritted her teeth, twisted her fingers together, did everything she could think of to keep from throwing the silver candelabra at Margaret. Her sister's eyes narrowed, and she took two quick puffs at her cigarette.

'Scored a direct hit, did I,' she laughed. 'You've been married all this time and you still haven't been in his bed? Poor baby.'

Mary struggled to control herself. Her sister's guess had struck her at her weakest point. Think of all the varied reasons why you haven't been in Harry's bed, she told herself. All the excuses, covering only one reason. You were afraid. Not of Harry. Afraid of crossing the line into womanhood. But now—perhaps it's too late. With Margaret here, will Harry wait?

'You said—if I'm not careful, Margaret. What did you mean by that?'

'Simple, dunce. Just tell me where it is, and we won't have to fight over Harry. After all, I don't really *want* to have him lording it over me. Just tell me where it is.'

'Where what is?'

'Don't act stupid. Dad turned everything he owned into cash and diamonds before my—your wedding. Seven-hundred-and-fifty-thousand dollars. I've been searching Boston madly, and haven't found it. If you help me get my hands on the money, you can keep Harry, with my blessings. It's really my money, you know. *I* was his daughter—his heir.'

'I don't know where it is,' Mary sighed. 'I haven't even thought about it. Maybe the police have it. Most of that was crooked money, Margaret.'

'So what! It spends just as easy, and it's mine!' Anger was sharpening her face, giving her the look of a vixen ready to bite. Mary backed away from the aura of hatred that pulsed at her, not knowing what to do next.

'I'll try to find out,' she gulped at last. 'In the meantime, you can stay with us. I've put you in the Bronze suite on the second floor. Dinner will be at six-thirty, if you can stand home-cooked spaghetti?'

'You have a good cook?'

'Of course. Me.'

Margaret broke out into a wild, almost hysterical laugh. 'You? You're married to one of the richest men in Boston, and you cook your own dinner? What are you trying to prove?'

'Nothing. I'm not trying to prove anything. Harry would hire five cooks if I asked him to—but I prefer it this way. Besides, Penny has to learn her way around in a kitchen, too, and there's no better teacher than her own mother.'

'Stepmother, you mean. You must be the most naive girl in the city. Cooked spaghetti! But then you always were the domestic, weren't you? I never ever stirred a finger in the kitchen, and look where it's got me!'

'Yes.' Mary struggled to suppress the sarcasm in her voice. Look where it's got you, indeed, Margaret. Here you are begging in my home, without a visible talent to your name. And I learned to cook and sew and keep house and teach school. And look where it's got me!

'Well, don't expect me to join you for supper. I need to regain contact with my old crowd. Which reminds me, I need some money.'

'I've got fifty dollars,' Mary offered. 'From the household accounts.'

'Fifty dollars? You must be mad. That's hardly

enough to keep me in taxi fares. And besides that, you'll have to see about my bill at the Sheraton.'

'It's not much, but that's the best I can do,' Mary snapped. 'I don't use a great deal of money. Harry pays for everything.'

'All right. I'll talk to Harry. Right now I need a rest. It's been a hectic day. Don't forget what I told you. Find Dad's money if you want to keep Harry.'

'Come off it, Margaret,' she responded. 'You sound like an old-time melodrama. I'll do my best for you, but you'd better be sure that you leave Harry and Penny alone!'

She explained it all in detail to Harry that night, while Penny was enjoying a bath under Mrs Hudley's eye. That is, she explained everything except the part about Margaret reclaiming *him*. For some reason, that stuck in her throat. And even when Harry pressed her she kept it to herself.

'I'll take care of her hotel bill,' Harry concluded, 'and provide her with a little pocket money. I'll also contact a few friends internationally and see what we can find out. But don't count on anything, Miss Mary. Now, before your eyes fall out of your pretty head, why don't you hustle upstairs and get to bed.'

'You'll be along soon?' she pleaded. 'I'm really not all *that* tired.'

He seemed to hesitate, searching for just the right words. 'I can't, love,' he finally said. 'I have two errands tonight. One is a schedule I swore I would keep up. The other is for Margaret.'

The words echoed through her head. The other is for Margaret! She's been here but one day, and already he has to do something for Margaret! Is this the first step on the way out? It couldn't be. Not possible!

'You have to take Margaret someplace?' She hadn't wanted to ask, but it had slipped out of her mouth unbidden. And as soon as it was out she covered her ears. She didn't want to hear the answer. 'No, don't tell me!' She sealed his lips with the palm of her hand. 'Don't tell me. I don't want to know!'

'Okay,' he chuckled. 'I won't tell you. Incidentally, I had a long talk with Penny when I took her up this afternoon. She's so excited she can't stand still. We'll talk about it tomorrow when we go on our trip.'

Immediately the dull ache in her heart disappeared. 'We're going on a trip? Just you and me?'

'Just you and me and Penny,' he retorted. 'Did I forget to tell you?'

'I—maybe I wasn't listening,' she offered as a sort of apology.

'So I'll say it again,' he laughed. 'Tomorrow is the Fourth of July. The Birthday of the Nation, and all that. And tomorrow night the Boston Pops Orchestra will present their annual concert on the Esplanade.'

'Oh, Harry! And we can go see it—hear it. Whatever?' She was so excited that she burrowed up against him and put her arms around his waist. 'I've always wanted to go, but they have such crowds, and I——'

'No crowds for us,' he said, damping her enthusiasm as if he had poured a pail of ice-water over her head.

'No? We can't go?' She was almost in tears again. Back and forth, she told herself. He's got me operating like a yo-yo. Up one minute, down the next. I don't understand him. I don't understand me!

'Oh, we're going,' he said. 'But not in the crowds. They expect two hundred thousand people tomorrow. Space will be filled by six o'clock, easily. And when it's over, the lucky ones will still be trying to get home by three in the morning.'

'So?'

'So, the Esplanade is a strip of grassland between Storer Drive and the Charles River Basin. We own a boat. Tomorrow we will get in our boat, go downstream to the proper area, and anchor there. We listen to the music, spend the night on our boat, and come home in the morning. Okay?'

'I—heaven's yes,' she sighed happily. 'I think I'd better go upstairs. Have a good time tonight, love.' She tried to sound casual about it all, but when she stretched up to kiss him, all her pretence disappeared.

The touch of his lips was a spark that fired her spirits, rattled the cage where her psyche was penned up, and almost utterly destroyed the narrow parochial upbringing of the oldest of the McBain girls. When he released her she ran for the stairs.

'I really *do* have to go, Miss Mary,' he called up after her, and all through the night she treasured the sound of regret buried deep in his voice.

Everybody overslept on the Fourth of July. It was a sultry humid day, under the influence of a Bermuda High. Mary woke up with a choking feeling, to see herself in the big bed in the master bedroom. The pillow next to her was dented, but empty. She smiled ruefully at herself. So you finally decided to come to him, she chastised herself, and then you fell asleep before he even got here. If he did get here? Had he really come? And if so, had he—oh lordy. It couldn't possibly happen and I wouldn't even know? Damn! Damn! She struggled out of bed and made a mad dash for the bathroom.

Twenty minutes later she walked into Penny's room, to find the girl also just waking up. 'The mask works fine,' she laughed. As she swung her feet out of the bed, she lifted the black lace mask from over her eyes. 'Oooooooh!' she exclaimed.

Mary turned from where she had been picking up discarded clothing. 'Something wrong dear?'

'I don't think nothin's wrong,' the child returned happily. 'You got black hair, Mommy. And a green blouse?'

'Penny! And so I have, sweetheart!' She hugged the child close, and then twirled her around as her daddy loved to do.

'Hey, I might break,' the child complained. But she was laughing as she did so. 'I don't see real clear, but I see you! And that's what I've always wanted to see. Is it really black?'

'It's really black, baby. What else can you see?'

'Well, nothing, really. Your face is a sort of blur, and your blouse is green—and you're wearing brown slacks!

But that's more than yesterday. And my head doesn't hurt!'

And with that good news they went downstairs, where Harry had been at the telephone for three hours. After breakfast he sent Penny off, and escorted Mary into the study. 'We've had some luck,' he reported. 'Your father's personal effects—the things he had in his pockets, are being sent by air. They've found his wallet, keyring—that sort of thing. It should be here tomorrow sometime. And the news about Penny is a real miracle—you were right, there's no other name to call it. We'll celebrate today. Did you invite Margaret to go with us?'

Mary blushed. 'I—I didn't—I——' she stammered. 'I was going to wait. If she gets up in time, I thought I might ask her. No, Harry, that's not true, and I don't want to lie to you—ever. I didn't ask her because I don't want her to go with us. This is a family affair—the Richardson family.' The last sentence came out with more determination, more spirit. He chuckled at her embarrassment. 'That's my girl,' he said.

As it happened, there was no conflict. Margaret came down at noon with her day already planned. So the Richardsons set of at four o'clock, loaded with chicken and sun-lotion and dark glasses and laughter.

The boat was moored at a little dock just up the river from the Massachusetts Institute of Technology's campus. It was a graceful twenty-five foot long catamaran, a sailboat with two narrow hulls joined together by pylons and pinions. A flat canvas deck was stretched over a frame above the hulls, and a low canvas cabin, somewhat on the order of a flatroofed tent with windows, was carefully fitted under the stick that——

'Boom,' he interrupted her. 'It's not a stick. It's called a boom, and it holds the bottom of the sail.'

'Okay,' she muttered half to herself. 'Boom. Crazy language. Sounds more like a shooting gallery.'

'It's a shallow-draft gaff-rigged non-polluting boat,'

he raved on. 'Just what we need in the Basin. And you're the crew.'

'Who me?' Mary squeaked in alarm. 'The only other boat I've ever been on is the Swanboat at the Public Gardens.'

'So you'll learn,' he shrugged. 'Everybody wears a lifebelt. Penny also wears a tether. You can swim?'

'Like a fish,' she replied mournfully. 'At least for fifty feet. After that, like a stone.'

'So you'll——'

'I know—so I'll learn.'

'Hey. Don't ever interrupt the Captain. Cast off that line aft.'

'Do what to who?'

'That line at the back of the boat—aft. Look, you have to learn.' There was a yachtsman's sarcasm for a lubberly crew in his tone, and Mary felt mildly insulted.

'You mean that rope in the back that holds us to the pier?'

'Yes,' he sighed. It was a somewhat exaggerated sigh that sent Penny into spasms of giggles. 'Now look,' he insisted. 'This is a sheet, that is a line, and those are halliards. Got it?'

'They all look like ropes to me,' she said indignantly. 'Why do you have all this nautical gibberish? Is it because sailors can't speak plain English? I hate that when people invent their own languages. The doctors do it, the lawyers, the engineers, and now the sailors. No wonder our kids are functionally illiterate!'

'Okay,' he sighed, genuinely this time. 'Okay, I know when I'm licked. We'll do it your way. But only for this trip, mind you!'

'Yes sir, Captain Bligh sir,' she snapped.

'Don't be a wise guy. Hold this—rope—while I go forward and cast off!'

There was a gentle following wind blowing right down the channel. He took them down the north bank as far as the Charles River dam, the structure that created the huge water basin. They stopped just off the Longfellow bridge to watch while the Harvard rowing eight ran their practice sessions on the mirror-like surface of the basin. In the fading light their racing shells looked like eight-oared centipedes, straddling their way up river.

As dusk began to settle in he tacked back upriver and across to the south bank, where they dropped anchor just off the Embankment, a dozen metres north of the Hatch Shell, the giant clam-shell stage where the musicians were to play.

After he stowed everything away he came aft and joined the girls on the canvas deck. He dropped down to a sitting position, his back against the cabin wall. 'Now, I've done my part,' he announced.

'And that, Penny,' Mary explained, 'is the dominant male!'

'It is not,' the little girl argued. 'That's just Daddy. Now what does he want?'

'He wants us famales to serve and pamper him,' Mary chuckled.

'You wouldn't dare say that if we were alone, would you,' he grunted. 'Would you?'

'No—I—no. I don't suppose I would,' she returned honestly. 'I'm not all that brave yet.'

'That's better,' he laughed. 'A little honest servility—humbleness—that's what I like in my women. Now, I want you both to come over here and kiss me, and then I'll have my supper.'

They sat in companionable silence after the meal. There was a constant hum in the air, the result of one hundred thousand people conversing quietly on the grass. The lights were gleaming in the high-rise buildings downtown. A faint gleam of a rising moon lit a path across the harbour. Mary was suddenly swept up in a shivering moment of exultation. The city is before me, the music waits, and here I am *with my family*! She turned her head slightly to encompass the other two. Penny was flat on the deck, her glasses off, with her father's head close beside her. 'It's a star, baby. Can you really see it?'

'Yes. Yes I can, Daddy. They look as close as the

treetops, don't they?' But the rest of the conversation was drowned out in the swelling crash of music, as John Williams lifted his baton and led the orchestra into his own composition, the theme of *Star Wars*. It seemed as if the cars on the highway, the subway trains on their noisy tracks, the entirety of Beantown had stopped to listen. And in minutes, before the piece was completed, Penny was fast asleep.

'I'll put her in the cabin,' Harry said softly. 'I bet she won't move for the rest of the night.' He required Mary's assistance, in the end. The cabin was only high enough for kneeling, not standing. Together, they managed to slide the child into her sleeping bag. She had not stirred a muscle. 'That's your bag.' He indicated a second sleeping bag at the other end of the cabin.

'And where are you sleeping?' And the minute the words were out she bit at her stupid lip. It was the last subject she wanted to raise—where was he going to sleep!

'Out there,' He gestured to a double-width bag on the open deck. 'And now hush up,' he commanded. He seated them both side by side, leaning back against the cabin wall, with his arm around her shoulders. She squirmed closer to him, and savoured the sheer contentment. The music shifted to a Chopin theme. The comfort of his arm, the swell of the music, the soft coolness of the tiny breeze that flicked through her hair, all conspired to send her mind off into the world of *what if*, daydreaming by moonlight. Her world, except for the burr that was Margaret, was all in tune. They had wound up the problem of Jim McBain, and relieved her slim shoulders of a burden carried too long. Penny was slowly but surely regaining her sight. And she had Harry. Or is it he had her? Have her? It wasn't just gratitude that was sweeping her tiny frame. She knew that, although she did not know how she knew. It was more than kindness. It was more than—lust. It was just a mad driving impulse to become part of him, to give him the one gift she had to give! But how does *he* feel? I wonder if I dare? She picked up the big hand that rested lightly on her shoulder, and tugged it down until it cupped her breast. It lay still. He isn't paying any attention, she thought disgustedly. But then somehow the hand moved, flicked aside the buttons on her blouse and slipped within, where it squeezed gently, and teased at her wildly erect peak. She shivered, losing all contact with reality, except for that one point of contact where his warm hand gently treasured her softness!

It took a sudden crash from all around her to shake her out of her dream. She was so startled that she jumped out of his arms, only to be pulled back close again.

'That will teach you to sleep on the Pops,' he laughed.

'I wasn't sleeping,' she protested, 'just day-dreaming. What was all that noise?' She searched the horizon uneasily.

'It's the regular annual conclusion to the performance, the 1812 Overture. Watch the fireworks from the bridge.'

'But I'm sure I heard guns!'

'Of course you did. They're written in the score. And there's one of the batteries of the Massachusetts National Guard over on the north bank. When the music calls for cannons in Boston, cannons we get. Look at that sky rocket go!'

She ooohed and aaaahed with the crowd for another thirty minutes before the sounds died away, the rockets flared out in the water, and the lights began to dim at the Hatch Shell.

'And now appreciate your position,' he chuckled. 'There are a hundred thousand people out there in the dark, all trying to find their way home. And us, we're going to stay at anchor here until daylight. Get to bed, Mrs Richardson.'

He gave her a supporting boost to her feet, and she struggled into the cabin. As she stripped for the night she could hear him squirming as he made himself comfortable out on the deck. She had brought pyjamas, but suddenly decided not to wear them. She sat down on her own bedroll, unwilling to climb inside, because that would be a commitment. Her blood was on fire, her mind straining to picture what he was doing out on the deck. Sleeping, she told herself disgustedly. And there is all that moonlight, and he's a virile man. And he's my husband. And I want him. God how I want him! And he's just out there—sleeping! How can he be sleeping when I want him so badly! Her passions drove her out of the cabin on her hands and knees. She stood up behind him, a pale picture of passion, the silver moon bathing her nudity, sparkling off the roseate peaks of her tortured breasts, shivering as the night-wind caressed her flank.

'Mr Richardson,' she called in a husky tormented voice.

His bedroll stirred as he sat up, displaying his own nudity, like Apollo waiting for his bride. 'What is it,' he asked. 'Something on fire?'

'Yes,' she whispered. 'Me!' All thought had fled from her mind, buried by the mad drive to offer herself to this man. She stood for just a second, frozen in marble, long hair draped carelessly around her, a sweet mesmerised smile on her face. He said nothing, but flipped back the edge of his bedroll, and extended a hand to her. Still without speaking, she slipped into the warmth, into the comfort, and forgot the entire world.

She lay still at his side for a moment, then slid over gently until they were touching, thigh to thigh, her tender breasts crushed against him. She felt that shiver again, the monumental ping of excitement that seemed to begin at his first touch. His hand gently threaded her hair, smoothing the dark silkiness of it around her head. Gently, ever so gently, his teeth nibbled at her earlobe, followed the line of her throat, sealed her mouth with his, probing, sensing, as his hand stroked her shivering body. One of his legs crossed over hers, pinning her in his grasp, as his hands climbed up from the pit of her stomach, up the hill of her breasts, and stopped there, teasing, before moving down again, lower than before, and repeated the trip. For long moments he teased her, encouraged her, drove her tensions higher and higher until she was panting, begging, pleading. For a minute longer he traced the flame of his mouth down across her nipples, and then, as gentle as a quiet flame, he moved between her legs and took her with him on a wild trip up to the gates of Olympus, and through.

It took her a long time, lying in the circle of his arms, to regain her breath, and to control her emotions. 'I—I never dreamed—that—I never dreamed it would be like that! Never! I love you, Harry.'

'Don't be too sure of that,' he chuckled. 'Maybe it was just plain old-fashioned lust. Did I hurt you?'

Did I hurt you? I've never felt so good in all my life, she told herself. So maybe there was a flash of pain, at the very beginning. Just plain old-fashioned lust? Well—just because I've fallen in love with him, doesn't necessarily mean he's fallen in love with me! He needs a wife. He needs a mother for his daughter. And a son to go with it. But that doesn't mean he loves me. Just plain old-fashioned lust! 'But if that's all I can get, I'll take it,' she said aloud.

'You'll what? Are you talking to yourself again?'

'I said, if I could find a shower right now, I'd take it,' she lied.

'No shower, but the biggest cold bath you ever had,' he chuckled. He squirmed out of the sleeping bag, scooped her up in his arms, and stepped off the side of the boat. The water closed over her head before she had a chance to think, but his arms held her tight, and brought her back to the surface squealing, her teeth chattering.

'Sssssh,' he admonished. 'You'll wake Penny.' She clung to the side of the boat, brushing the hair out of her eyes, kicking her feet against him to keep him at a respectable distance. But he was having none of that. Those cable-like arms enclosed her again, and as they sank under the surface his lips sealed hers. For a moment he held her under, then released her. She bobbed to the surface, giggling, and vaulted back on to the boat before he could catch up to her. And then he chased her forward to the bow, back around on the starboard side, making threatening and obscene suggestions, she squealing as she ran. Until suddenly a light flared just off their stern, and a small cabin cruiser could be seen.

'What the hell,' the words came clearly over the water. 'Either bed her or throw her overboard!'

Mary collapsed, soaking wet, on the deck adjacent to the sleeping bags. In a second he pounced on her. At first it seemed a continuation of the game, frivolous, enjoyable. But suddenly its tenor changed as his hand swept across her breast again. Immediately he pulled her back against him, discarded all thought of gamesmanship, and began that sensual massage that so aroused her. It took only a minute for her to reach the peak of desire again, and all that time she could feel the hardness of his aroused muscles playing against her. Until finally it all went beyond her control. 'Now. Please! Now!' she begged.

He swept her up in his arms and carried her over to the warmth of the padded bedroll, dropping her into the middle of it, and falling beside her as she fell. Her uncontrollable hands roamed over him at will, fluttered at him, tested his arousal. 'Please!' she begged. And he proceeded to demonstrate, in tantalising detail, that the second time around can often be sweeter than the first. She squealed at the climax, a long-drawn-out salute, until, from the adjacent boat, a tired male voice said, 'For God's sake!' It was like being doused with a pail of water. Harry rolled to one side, still holding her. She giggled into his shoulder, doing her best to smother the sound. He squeezed her gently.

'Did that do it,' he whispered in her ear. 'Are all your ghosts well and truly laid?'

'I don't know about ghosts,' she whispered back, 'but I am!'

'You am what?'

'I am well and truly——'

'Hush,' he snapped, putting a hand over her mouth. 'Nice girls don't talk like that!' He shifted his weight and pulled her close into his protective arms. And then they slept.

CHAPTER NINE

'SHE'S been here six weeks now,' Mrs Hudley complained. 'How much longer do you expect she'll stay?' The two of them were sitting in the kitchen having a nine-o'clock cup of coffee.

'I don't know,' Mary admitted. 'I thought at first it would be just a few days, but now—I just don't know. I think she brought everything she owns, don't you?'

'If you mean by way of luggage, I agree.' Mrs Hudley took a sip from her cup and looked at the forlorn figure across the table. 'You're not taking care of yourself. Every time your sister comes downstairs she's dressed to kill. Look at your hair. And that sloppy dress!'

'I—I just don't seem to feel very well in the mornings anymore,' Mary protested weakly. 'And I—I don't think I need to compete with my own sister. Why should I?'

'So it's all true what I heard.' Mrs Hudley nodded sagely. 'You're too good to be a McBain. Do you know something? When you first came into this house I thought you were pulling my leg—you'd never been here before, you said—you had only just met Harry. I really thought it was some kind of joke. I had seen you come in a dozen times before and sneak upstairs to the bedroom. And when your Miss Margaret waltzed in the door the other day I would have sworn it was you. But now I know better!'

I wish *I* knew better now, Mary thought. How could anything that started off so good have gone downhill so fast? Just six weeks ago, on the boat, it had been a wild awakening. And the two weeks that followed, sharing Penny's gradually regained sight, and Harry's bed! Paradise. And then quickly, as if someone had pulled the plug out of her bowl of contentment, everything had run out. Harry had become mysterious. Two nights a

150

week, and sometimes three, he was out late, 'working on an urgent project' was all he would tell her. And when he did come home he was just too tired to do more than shower and fall into bed, and quickly to sleep. Everything she had tried had failed—and heaven only knew how poor she was in the seduction line, even with her own husband. So, in the week just past, the next to the last week in August, she had come to accept it. Harry had made a judgment. His funtime was over. He didn't need her anymore. There was nothing left for her to do but bear up under it. After all, Penny still needed her, now more than ever.

But the thing that really hurt, the fact that she tried to hide from herself, was that every night Harry was out late, Margaret was too. Neither said a word about it. They didn't leave at the same time, nor come in at the same time, but—is it just my suspicious mind, she asked herself? From the beginning I thought my sister would try to steal my husband. Is that why I'm willing to make a numbed acceptance of it now?

'Miss Mary?' She looked up at her table companion. 'I said, I wonder what your sister really wants?'

She wants Harry, Mary felt like screaming! She wants everything I've got, but mainly she wants Harry! But it wasn't a confidence she wanted to share—even with Mrs Hudley. 'I really don't know,' she said instead, 'I suppose she came for the funeral, and just got here too late. And now she doesn't have any money, so she can't go anyplace else—if she had someplace else to go.'

'You don't suppose any such a thing!' Mrs Hudley was being purposefully rude. 'Stop daydreaming. If you want to keep Harry, you have to fight for him. You don't think we haven't all noticed that he's been out late two or three times a week lately? And don't give me that business about how Margaret was too late for the funeral. You know darn well she was at the Sheraton *before* the funeral!'

Why that was what Harry had said, and she had been too confused to pay attention! But—surely, as close as Margaret and Dad had been, she would have come to the funeral! There was bound to be a reasonable explanation—which she could get only if she asked.

'I'm sure she would have come if she could,' Mary said glumly. 'She loved Dad. He was more *her* father than mine.'

'Wake up, Miss Mary! Put off your rosy glasses. Your sister is deeply in love with herself. Listen to that darn bell ring. What do you suppose she wants now?'

'Breakfast, I suppose. Why don't you make up a tray and I'll take it up to her.'

'Why don't we both just sit here and let her come down for her breakfast? Is she too hoity-toity to mingle with us peasants?'

'Please, Mrs Hudley!' Mary threw up her hands defensively. 'I can't take any more of this. I just can't! If it will keep the peace, I'll take her breakfast up to her on my hands and knees!'

'And if it will keep the peace, you'll let her take Harry?'

'No!' she shouted. 'That's different! And please don't talk like that. Please?'

'All right, love. Here. The eggs are a little overdone, but they'll serve. And be careful. The coffee pot is heavy. Are you sure you want to take this up?'

It *was* heavy. Far heavier than Mrs Hudley could have imagined, because it carried not only Margaret's breakfast, but all of Mary's worries and tribulations. She opened the bedroom door by backing into the room. Her sister was sitting up in the middle of the big bed.

'Oh, it's you!' There was nothing welcome about Margaret's greeting. This was the first time in several weeks that they had been alone together. 'Well, I wanted to talk to you anyway.'

'And I want to talk to you,' Mary sighed as she slumped into a chair by the window, the tray on a table beside her. 'How long do you intend to impose yourself on us, Margaret?'

'Impose myself?' Her sister was laughing behind that mask of a face. 'Well, I really don't have anyplace else to go, do I? Daddy sold the old house, and I don't have two pennies to rub together. Surely you don't intend to throw me out on the street, do you?'

'Don't count on it,' Mary snapped. 'Too bad it doesn't snow at this time of year.'

'Now, now,' her sister trilled at her. 'Let's not say anything that could upset Harry, shall we? He wouldn't approve of his tender little wife acting bitchy.'

'Oh come off it,' Mary growled. 'Try telling me the truth for a change. Why did you come back? The real reason.'

'Why, you sent for me, as I recall.'

'We sent for you three days before the funeral. But you were already in Boston by then, weren't you? And why didn't you come to the funeral? He loved you. You know that.'

'Of course he did. Is that what makes you angry? That he loved me and not you?'

There was just enough truth in the accusation to sting. Mary turned away to hide the pain in her eyes. She nibbled at her lower lip, and demanded again, 'Why did you come?'

Margaret began to laugh. 'I told you that, too. My Portuguese Duke turned out to be a fake. Can you imagine that? So I just had to come home.'

'Only you don't have a home to come to, do you?'

Margaret instantly sobered. 'No I don't,' she said hoarsely. 'Because you stole it from me, little Miss Prim. You stole it from me, husband and all! And if I don't get Dad's money pretty soon, I'm going after Harry's. You'd better get busy, *sister*.'

Mary stumbled out of the bedroom, torn between rage and tears. Another five minutes with her sister and she would have broken down and cried a million gallons of tears. After which she would have bundled Margaret up and thrown her out the second-floor window, smile and all! I could plead temporary insanity, she told herself. A wry smile played around her lips as she considered her criminal past. I wonder which is worse, she thought, murdering my sister, or biting a policeman? You'd better get busy, sister. Indeed! She was still talking to herself as she stumbled up the stairs to the family quarters, showered, and crammed herself into her sedate navy blue suit. The one with the high collar and the pleated skirt.

'Where are you going, Mom?' Penny stood at the door. A very assured, confident Penny, wearing a stylish set of glasses that still changed from clear to dark depending upon the amount of light around her. A Penny who could not yet read with her eyes, but could distinguish shapes and forms and colours—and thank God, people.

'I'm going downtown to see your father,' she said, then remembered to smile. How many things had changed in the house now that Penny could see again!

'Can I come?'

'I—I don't see why not, dear. It's something very special I have to talk to him about. A sort of secret, you know. But you could wait with his secretary for a few minutes.'

'Something special? Oh great! You're going to have a baby!'

'Now, Penny——' she stuttered, flustered by the child's obvious pleasure in the thought. 'It's too early to tell. I only went to see the doctor three days ago. It's something else—another secret. Have you done all your studies?'

'Yeah, but it's boring,' the little girl replied. 'You know, it's harder for me to read Braille now than it used to be.'

Mary's heart turned over with a thump. Poor little lovable child, caught up in transition between two worlds. 'I'm sure it must be, love,' she returned gently, 'but very soon you will be up to grade level, and Daddy is considering sending you to a regular school. Give us a hug now, will you?'

The hug and the affection that went with it was strong enough to last through the cab ride downtown. Their driver was a young man of Japanese extraction, whose father evidently had been a Kamikaze pilot. He wasn't too pleased, either, with the size of the tip she left him. But she saw no reason why she should tip lavishly for his having put her life at risk! All of which disgorged the Richardson girls into the lobby of the vast office building, not a little upset.

They had their pick of lifts, since it was past the rush hour. Mary held on tightly to Penny's hand as the express machine shot upward. To overcome her fear she talked herself back in shape. Mrs Richardson, that's the ticket. Be Mrs Harry Richardson. Demand the red carpet. Strike up the trumpets. My lord's consort has come among you! And let's hope that 'my lord' doesn't break my neck for intruding on his business day! Which seemed such a ridiculous thought that when the lift doors opened she was giggling her fool head off. The receptionist was suitably impressed.

'Let me get you a messenger, Mrs Richardson.' It sounded so nice. She smiled a sweet acknowledgement, aware that Penny was clinging to her skirt and watching all the goings-on with wide eyes. Briefly thereafter they followed the nice young man down the corridor, around two bends, and there was Harry, leaning against the wall, waiting for them.

'Daddy!' Penny slipped her leash and ran down the hall, to be swallowed up and tossed ceiling high by her Viking father. Mary stopped a few feet away, and glowed as she watched them. He might have changed his mind about *her*, but his daughter was still the centre of his universe. If only there was room there for Mary Richardson, she thought wistfully. If only he—her thoughts flew out of her head as he set his daughter down on her dancing feet, and turned his attention to his wife. With the same exuberance he seized her about the waist, almost spanning her circumference with his hands, and then twirled her around and up, but only an inch or two. When he caught her startled frame in those gentle hands he was puffing, but laughing too. 'I'm getting better,' he announced proudly. I haven't the slightest idea what he's talking about, Mary told herself, but I wish he would do it again. The feeling of depression that had haunted her all morning disappeared.

'Well, now. This is the first time you've ever visited our establishment. With a little more warning I could have turned out the guard for inspection!'

'I been here before, Daddy.'

'I know *you* have, baby, but your mother never has. Until now, that is.' He grabbed at Mary again, twirled her around three times, and tossed her up somewhat higher than before. She shrieked—until his hands closed safely on her again. Heads were peering out of all the doors along the corridor. She tugged at her suit, doing her best to restore her dignity.

'You talk and act a lot of nonsense,' she observed. 'Are you sure you're the Mr Richardson who is the investment banker?'

'The very one,' he chuckled, pulling her into the inner office, past the desks of four giggling secretaries. 'I'll tell you what, little lady. We'll run an identity check.' Up in the air she went again, hoisted in his arms, where he proceeded to kiss her very thoroughly, very lovingly. 'How's that?' He set her back on her feet again. 'Proof positive?'

She leaned back to look up into his sparkling eyes. 'Yes,' she sighed contentedly. And then, as an afterthought, 'Yes sir!' It doesn't matter about Margaret, she told herself fiercely. It doesn't matter that he might only be having a good time. Right here and right now he's mine! She clutched at his arm and strolled into his inner sanctum, fumbling for composure. Inner Sanctum? Like an old-time radio programme? Well, it looks like a sanctum, she told herself. Three huge windows, letting in all the sun, blocking out all the polluted air. A thick brown carpet, whose nap almost reached her ankles. Five modernistic chairs. One clear desk.

'Is this where you work?' she puzzled. 'I don't see— where do the people come to make deposits and withdrawals?'

'It's not that kind of a bank,' he laughed. 'Say, I

didn't notice before, but what this office needs is a great big soft comfortable couch. Especially if my wife is going to call on me in the middle of the day!'

'No such thing,' she snapped, folding herself into one of the chairs. 'Go sit at your desk. There's where you belong. I have something terribly important to talk about.'

'Oh wow!' He did a slow Indian dance around the desk. 'Let me guess. You're going to have a baby?'

'She said no when I asked her, Daddy,' Penny interrupted. 'You told me she knew how to get one, but I don't think she does. She went to that old doctor, and she still don't know. She don't got no 'sperience.'

'No!' She shouted at both of them. They stopped teasing her, and waited expectantly. 'No. At least, I don't think so. You and your daughter have one-track minds!'

'You're really not?' he asked, crestfallen.

'Well, how can I be sure, she said, trying to cheer him up. 'I only saw the doctor a few days ago. These tests take time.'

'And that's not what you want to talk to me about?'

'No. Penny, why don't you go out and talk to Mrs Padfort for a while. I want to talk to your dad about a secret.' The little girl made a face, but started for the door. He must have pushed a button, because before Penny reached the door, it opened and his secretary took the little girl in hand.

'Okay,' he said, moving around to settle into his official chair. 'Now, I'm wearing my official banker's head. Speak, woman!'

Now that it was the time and the place, Mary could not quite bring herself to speak. She fumbled with the catch on her purse, rubbed the back of her right ankle with her left toe, glanced around at the view from the window, and finally took the plunge. 'It's Margaret,' she sighed.

His face dropped about five miles. 'Oh hell!'

'Yes, well——' she was anxious—no, determined—to get the issue settled, but was not quite sure how to go about it without setting off his awesome temper. 'We're at an impasse,' she said quietly. 'I want her to leave. She says she can't because she hasn't any money, and no home to go to. And it all comes back to this. Where's Papa's money?' She folded her hands in her lap and sat up straight, waiting for the fire-storm to follow. But nothing happened.

He leaned back in his swivel chair, twirling a pencil between his fingers. 'I know a little more than before.' He pulled open the middle drawer of his desk and took out a plain brown envelope.

'Your father's wallet.' He tossed it on the desk in front of her. 'Two sets of keys. A wristwatch. And his glasses. And that's all.'

'Is there anything in the wallet?' She leaned forward, feeling a small twinge of excitement building up. He shook his head.

'Not money, if that's what you mean. A gasoline credit card. A wallet picture of Margaret—or you. And this.' He drew out a tiny bit of well-folded paper.

'What is it?'

He held up a hand for patience as he carefully unfolded the paper. Scrawled across it was a number. Below it was a word in German. She slumped back in her chair, let down by the ordinary nature of it all.

'It's the number of a Swiss bank account,' he said. 'The word is a recognition-key. Your father apparently sent half his cash to this account, turned most of the rest into diamonds, and took off. I suspect he intended to make a deal with the drug runners. The diamonds haven't been seen since.'

'Then—this money in Switzerland. Could Margaret claim it?'

'Anybody who has the number and the code can claim it. Somebody already has. The entire account was paid over to an unidentified claimant in Bogota three days ago.'

She slumped back in the chair, depressed. 'So there's nothing,' she whispered, 'and no solution to my problem.'

'That's only partly true,' he returned. 'This key is the last hope. It's for a safe deposit box in the First Federal.'

Her spirits were instantly restored. 'That's something! What's in it?'

He looked at the eager expression in her eyes, the half-smile that changed her from an ordinary woman into one of spectacular beauty. A woman who had suffered so many knocks and bruises in her short life, and carried so many burdens for others. A woman who meant more to him than he could say. And he didn't have the heart to tell her that the box was empty.

'I don't know what's in it,' he lied. 'I've not had a chance to investigate. It's hard to get into a safe deposit box. Your father and Margaret were the only signatories to the account. I'll pick her up and take her over there as soon as possible.'

'Do you have to do it?' she asked wistfully. 'You couldn't send somebody?'

He shook his head slowly back and forth. 'She's family, Miss Mary. I'll take her.'

'Yes—I—I see that. Of course.' She stood up, smoothing down her skirt as she did so. Stop me, her heart was crying. Don't let me just walk away like this. Stop me! His blond hair was glistening in the reflected sunlight, outlining the profile of his strong chin, and those crazy tufts in the middle of his eyebrows.

'You couldn't stay to have lunch with me?' She hesitated, wanting madly to accept, and yet—and while she debated, the buzzer on his intercom buzzed at them and ruined her day. 'Miss Margaret McBain on line four,' his secretary said. 'She wants to remind you of your luncheon date. I managed a reservation for you at the NoName Restaurant.'

And so much for that, Mary told herself as she walked quickly to the door. 'Mary!' He called after her, but she closed the door firmly behind her, snatched up a surprised Penny, and marched smartly back to the lifts.

The two girls stopped at the house briefly for a bowl

of soup and a sandwich, and then went off on a walk. It was their first excursion since the accident. The child was over-excited, following with her newfound senses all the trails they had trod before in darkness.

'The fire hydrant!' She was doing a little jig around the squat public servant. 'Mickey the Squirter! Just like you said, Mommy. It's wonderful!'

Indeed it is, little girl, Mary thought. All wonderful. Life must seem so simple to you. Why does it have to be so complicated as we grow older? He's taking Margaret to lunch. So he invited me too—after he had forgotten Margaret. And then I suppose wanted me to come along as an afterthought. As if I would want to share him at lunch with Margaret! As if I want to share him at all! Lordy, how did I get so fiercely possessive?

'Mommy?'

'Yes, dear?' The little girl had stopped dead in her tracks, her brow furrowed.

'Mommy. My stomach feels—funny. I think I'm going to throw up.'

Thankful that they were only a few steps from home, Mary steered her back to the house and up the stairs. The child's cheeks were flushed. Mary took her temperature, re-checked the reading to be positive, and ushered the child to bed. 'You have a little fever, honey,' she told the child. But as soon as she settled the girl down in bed, she went downstairs to call Dr Burton.

'Dinner for two tonight,' she called to Mrs Hudley as she went by the kitchen. But even that was optimistic. When she came back downstairs the housekeeper met her at the dining-room door.

'Dinner's ready any time,' she reported, 'but the Mister called to say he won't be in for a meal.'

'Did he say why?'

'He said something about he had to take Miss Margaret to look at something. That's all I know.'

Five o'clock in the afternoon, and he was taking Margaret to look at a safe deposit box? Come on now. Even her naive little mind could hardly swallow that.

Banks closed at two-thirty in the afternoon—sometimes at three. But—oh hell, she muttered under her breath. I'm getting hypersensitive. So she stumbled through supper, eating just enough to keep the housekeeper satisfied, and went back upstairs to have a good cry.

Harry came in around ten o'clock, alone. Mary was pacing the hall, waiting. He flung his jacket on to the coat rack and gathered her up like a bunch of grapes. 'Waiting up for me?' he enquired casually.

'Yes, of course,' she said softly. 'Where did you go?'

'I had to take Margaret someplace,' he said. 'It came up rather suddenly. I didn't have a chance to explain beforehand, and you were out when I called.'

'It doesn't matter,' she returned, fishing a tissue from the pocket of her robe. 'You've got something red on your cheek.' She wiped it off. No, it doesn't really matter, she told herself. Lipstick on his cheek is no big thing. Well, is it? He had to take my sister someplace. Is that any reason to be jealous? Shut up, she screamed at herself!

'There's something wrong with Penny,' she told him. 'She's got the 'flu. Dr Burton came and left some pills and some orders. She's very restless. I think I had better stay with her tonight.' And then, as an afterthought, 'Did you get something to eat?'

'Yes,' he reported. 'We stopped for a bite before Margaret went on to her party.'

Let me turn around so you can stab me in the back, she screamed deep within herself. Use a dull knife! Did you enjoy dining out with my sister? Whoever would think that love stories could be true? If I didn't love you so much I would murder you right here at the foot of your own stairs! But she managed to hold it all in, and escaped with a thin-lipped goodnight.

Penny was extremely restless during that night. Three separate times Mary had to get up to help. Once, going down to the kitchen for some cool liquid, she was surprised to find that she was not the only one up. Margaret was there too, dressed in an identical nightgown, and with her hair down.

'Penny's got the 'flu,' Mary told her. 'I'm spending the night with her. Did you have a good time?'

'The best,' her sister reported. She wore that cat-smile on her face, and licked her lips as if she had recently eaten. 'A marvellous man, your husband.'

'Of course,' Mary replied dully. 'The best in the world.'

They had nothing more to say to each other. Mary got the drink and a pair of straws, and took them back up. Margaret followed her out of the kitchen and up the first flight of stairs, and then lingered at the newel post, watching as Mary disappeared around the bend. Penny sucked at the cooling liquid for a moment, and then dropped off to sleep.

The next day was worse. Mary sat by the bedside, eyes half-closed, and watched the child toss and turn. Harry looked in for a minute, warned her to take care of herself, and went off to work. Dr Burton arrived at three in the afternoon. He was apparently dissatisfied at the progress being made. He augmented the pills with a shot, and warned Mary to take care of herself.

At dinner time, worn to a splinter, Mary gave up the idea of eating, and asked for a bowl of soup. Mrs Hudley brought it up, fussing as she made the stairs. 'A whole dinner I made—dinner for three. And nobody to eat a bite of it. Here's your soup. You want me to sit with the child while you eat?'

'No. No thanks,' Mary replied. 'Thank you for bringing the soup. Where did Harry go?'

'I don't know. He just didn't come home for dinner. And about an hour ago your sister received a phone call and off she went. Dressed to kill, that one. Eat your soup. You haven't had anything all day.'

'I know. I'll try to get a little more down, later. You had better get your rest. We don't want you exposed to influenza. The whole house would fall apart if you got sick!'

Mrs Hudley snorted and walked out. Mary set the half-empty soup bowl down on the bedside table and lay down, meaning to rest her eyes for a moment. It was

three o'clock in the morning when Penny woke her up.
The child was bathed in perspiration, so soaked that her
sheets needed to be changed. Mary bustled around with
eyes half-closed, but managed to complete the task.
Penny fell back on to the dry sheets in a dry nightie,
and was asleep almost immediately. Mary stood by the
bed for a time, watching, then went back to sleep
herself.

The first peep of dawnlight woke her up. The clock
on the side table said seven-thirty. She had slept for
four hours, was still tired and confused, but could not
drop off again. So she shrugged her way out of the light
sheet which covered her, fumbled for a robe, and
grumbled her way downstairs. Harry was having a last
cup of coffee in the kitchen. He caught and kissed her
as she wandered by, drawn by the smell of the coffee.

'Hey stranger,' he called. 'Good to see you!'

She poured herself a mug of the hot steaming brew,
and took a couple of tentative sips. 'I missed seeing you
last night,' she said flatly.

'I came home late,' he explained. 'I was working on a
project. When I did get in you were both fast asleep.'

'I guess I'm just a poor night watchman,' she said,
smiling at him. 'I was only going to rest my eyes for a
second.'

'Famous last words. How's Penny now?'

'Better. Much better. Her fever broke about three
o'clock this morning. I had to change her entire bed.
But then she fell asleep—a natural sleep, I mean. She's
still pounding her ear. I think we've survived the crisis.'

'I hope so,' he said solemnly. 'I've missed you.'

I've missed you. Four little words, but enough to
compensate for all the little suspicions, all the long
absences, all the heartaches. 'I've missed you too,' she
replied. He pulled her over against him. Standing beside
his seated form she could barely see the top of his head.
She kissed the edge of his scalp, and then squealed as he
grabbed at her. 'Watch my coffee!' she warned as she
broke away from him, cradling her mug in both hands.

'What do you need most, coffee or me?' he purred.

'At this moment, coffee,' she announced. 'Well, a husband is available every day, but a good cup of coffee is hard to find. And right now this coffee is my lifeline.'

She backed away from him, into a corner of the room, and sipped at the brew, watching him over the top of the mug with loving eyes. Why do I love him, she asked herself. Because I do, that's why. I don't really believe in Equal Rights. I just want to be yours, all the time. And if I were to tell you that right now? Dear Lord, I don't dare! That would be like Red Riding Hood inviting the Wolf in for lunch! 'Don't you have to go to work?' she asked.

'Well, that's a switch.' He finished off his coffee and got up, stretching slowly to full height. 'As it happens, I do,' he chuckled. 'I have a big deal on this morning. Otherwise, Mrs Richardson, you'd be in a lot of trouble.'

'It's nice to know where I rank,' she teased, dodging around the end of the table as he came after her. 'It's very important business?'

'Smart aleck,' he said. 'But I do appreciate the way you take care of my daughter.'

'Our daughter,' she corrected him. 'Will you be home for dinner tonight?'

'I'm not sure.' He was halfway to the door, briefcase in hand, and she willed him to stop. He did. 'If I can get things going right, I'll have everything settled tonight. Don't wait up.'

'You'll be out with Margaret?' she asked wistfully.

He looked at her for a long minute, then pulled her close and kissed her very satisfactorily. There were stars in her eyes as she watched him go. He hadn't said, but that kiss was answer enough, wasn't it?

Somehow or another, in between conferences with Mrs Hudley about getting the house back on schedule, she missed Margaret's breakfast time, and barely saw the back of her as she went out the front door. It seemed strange, as she thought about it, that Margaret would abandon her sophisticated hair style for something that favoured Mary's own. And when she went upstairs to dress, she had another uncomfortable feeling. Her favourite perfume bottle was missing.

But the little things that nagged her all vanished when Penny woke up at eleven. The child's temperature was down below one hundred degrees for the first time in three days. She was thoroughly dehydrated, weak, but alive and kicking. Mary managed a big smile, helped the little girl into the bath, and supervised a complete wash. While the two were playing in the bathroom, Mrs Hudley came in and changed all the bed linen again. When Penny returned to bed she looked a world different, and felt a universe better.

That afternoon all the ladies participated in the programme to stuff the child with liquids, and Mary gave her a long read from *Treasure Island* before the two of them faded out in an afternoon nap. At four o'clock Mary managed to wander downstairs again for a bowl of soup. She had just finished when Margaret came through the door, excited.

'Some of it was there!' she announced, and threw her arms around her sister's neck. 'It was there. I feel a million percent better!'

'What was there?' Mary asked.

'In the safe deposit box,' her excited sister said. 'Harry brought me the key, and we went down to the bank. And there it was. Twenty thousand dollars in cash. All mine!'

'I'm happy for you,' Mary smiled. 'That must take a load off your mind. Now what are your plans?'

Her sister, who was almost out of the kitchen by this time, looked back over her shoulder. 'Don't get your hopes up, Mary. It's a nice sum, but not enough to live on. I think I'll have Harry after all!' She was laughing as she went up the stairs. Mary could hear the shrill taunting trills until the kitchen door swung shut, locking out sight and sound.

Mary slumped down at the table, stunned. Once or twice her undirected hand dipped the spoon into the empty soup plate. Her mouth could not seem to realise that she was spooning air. I think I'll have Harry after all! Her ire began to rise. Damned if you will, her mind screamed. Damned if you will. If you want a fight, lady, you'll get it. The only thing that can send me off is Harry! But suppose he chose Margaret? She put it out of mind. He had not filled her ears with endearments, but his kiss this morning had said everything. Hadn't it?

It was a doggedly tired woman who took Penny's dinner up to her on a tray, and shared it with her. Margaret stuck her head around the door at eight, just as Penny was settling down again. It was the first time she had come near the sickroom since Penny had been taken ill.

'There isn't any dinner,' she complained.

'Yes, well, we're all tired, Margaret,' she returned. 'I thought you might just fend for yourself for one night.'

'Don't you ever get tired of wearing that nightgown?' her sister asked.

'This one?' Mary fingered the satin, and the lace inserts. 'Harry likes it. I thought you did too. You got yourself one just like it.'

'A classical mistake,' Margaret laughed. 'Are you spending the night with the girl?'

'She has a name. Penny. Not *the girl*. I've been spending every night with her since she came down sick.'

Margaret shrugged her shoulders and clumped downstairs in her wooden-heeled sandals. Without even a word to Penny, Mary mused. As if the child couldn't hear. How could anyone *not* love this little girl?

'You're talking to yourself again, Mommy.'

'So I am. You are getting to be a wonderful *looker*, aren't you?'

'I don't think there's a word like that. You made it up. Besides, I can hear you breathe when you talk to yourself. Don't you like Aunt Margaret?'

And how do you truthfully answer a question like that? 'She's my sister. My twin sister,' she improvised.

'That's not a fair answer,' the girl giggled.

'Maybe not, but it's the best you're going to get

tonight, pumpkin. Now go to sleep. By tomorrow you'll be a new woman.'

'Will I really, Mommy? What kind of new? Like Margaret?'

'Oh shut up,' her mother laughed. 'Just darn well shut up.'

She settled down in the other twin bed, shifting around to find the comfort she knew would never be there. The latest issue of the National Geographic was at the bedside, but she found herself reading the pictures and ignoring the prose. A wind had risen outside, and the old house was creaking. She heard Harry come in late. Her clock said eleven. At quarter to twelve he tiptoed in to check up on things. She felt almost as if she were cheating, being so wide awake, but she dropped the magazine on her breast and closed her eyes, feigning sleep. His footsteps came closer, circled both beds, and she felt a moist contact as he kissed her forehead and put away her book. And then he put out the light and went out.

Another hour passed. Sleep eluded her, tired as she was. Penny was sleeping with her mouth open, bubbling as she breathed, but there was a smile on her face, and she clutched her rag doll tightly in the crook of her arm. Everything seemed normal. Except for me, she sighed ruefully. Here I am, trying to sleep, when what I need is only fifty feet away, across the hall, behind closed doors. Penny is sleeping normally. Why shouldn't I steal a few hours off? The wish was parent to the deed.

She inched out of bed and into her felt slippers. The child turned over, but did not wake up. As quietly as she could, Mary pressed the *on* button on the electronic monitor, and ghosted out of the room. The hall was dark. The night-light that guarded the top of the stairs was out, and the windows at either end of the corridor were bringing in only a feeble light. She shrugged her shoulders. Driven by her needs, there was no reason to turn back just because the lights were out. Cautiously she felt her way along the opposite wall until her hand came to the depression that was the doorway into the master bedroom.

She stopped just long enough to pluck out the hairpins that constrained her mop of hair. It was one of the things he insisted on, having her soft silky hair loose by his pillow. She pulled back her shoulders, and reached for the knob. He would wake up in a cloud of hair this time, and hear something he might not expect. The medical report had come back from the laboratory in the late afternoon mail.

She palmed the knob and slowly opened the door. There was a spot at which the door squeaked, and not all Mr Hudley's oil-can skills had been able to solve the problem. With the door one-third open, she turned sidewise and squeezed in.

On this side of the house there was a little more light from the reflected moon. She could see the armchair where he always scattered his clothes, and where she always picked them up. She could see the light coverlet, thrown half on the floor, the way he usually did. She could smell, almost overwhelmingly, her own favourite perfume, which *she* was not wearing tonight. She backed up against the doorjamb to steady herself. There were two intertwined bodies spread across the bed, and he already had a mass of silky black hair resting on his pillow, mingling with his golden crown!

CHAPTER TEN

FOR the length of one skipped heartbeat Mary stood and stared. The pale moonlight cast an eerie sheen over the room, but there could be no mistake. There were two people in the bed, tumbled across each other, asleep. She fumbled behind her for support, unthinking, empty, confused. And then she succumbed to the flight syndrome. As cautiously as she had come in, she slipped out, closing the heavy door behind her. In the freedom of the corridor she breathed again, sagging against the wall as something inside her began to freeze, to chill her emotions, slow her reactions.

The old Chinese saying was true. One picture *is* worth a thousand words, and she had seen the picture. There was no need of explanation. The flash of silky black hair on the pillow had said it all. Dejection seized her, rended her mind, plummeted her spirits into depths she had never before conceived.

Slowly, on wavering legs, she made her way back to Penny's room and slipped into the security of the narrow bed. What to do? Bravado? Go downstairs, get Harry's shotgun, and shoot them both? Go in, drag her sister out by the hair, bump her down the stairs and out of the house? Let Harry try to explain? All dreams. She recognised that almost immediately. But it's hard to be logical when ravening wolves are tearing at your insides, stirring bile in the pit of your stomach. She struggled to keep from screaming her frustration. Battled to control herself. And finally did.

Once more she went back over her experience, but this time coldly, constructing syllogisms of ice to reason her way to a conclusion. And the first conclusion was indisputable. Harry had made a choice about the McBain twins. Leave Mary to watch the baby, and take Margaret to bed with him. Which seemed to say it all.

So what then? If he wanted Margaret, then Mary would have to go. What profit could it be to share a house with them? To eat her heart out watching from the sidelines? There was hardly any need to add up the score, the game was over. She sighed in disgust, and tried to nibble at her problem from another view.

But if I go—if I leave the field to Margaret, what about Penny. Did Penny deserve a stepmother like Margaret? Was the poor little love-starved girl equipped to survive in a family where Margaret would be her mother? No, of course not. Margaret might try to fake the love, for Harry's sake, but the little girl was too sharp for that. In fact, Penny would be better off with no mother at all, than to be saddled with Margaret.

And what of Harry? Did he deserve to be married for his money? He was a strong-willed man, and yet—there had been those times when he was also an enthusiastic boy—a charmer of hearts. And how badly he wanted a son. Would Margaret give him one? He was a man who liked a family life. Would *she* reform, give up her wild parties, her mad friends? Or would she drag him along with her down whatever path she was paving?

Mary wrestled with her problem for half the remaining night, and finally came to a bitter conclusion. For the sake of the two people she loved most in the world, she would have to take the drastic step. Clear the chess board of *all* the McBains, and leave Harry and Penny with each other, and a chance to start again!

'I'll do it!' she told the dark world around her. 'God give me strength.' And only then did she drop off into a troubled sleep.

When she awoke in the morning she was a woman totally changed. A wall of ice surrounded her heart, walled her from all assaults and passions. She forced a smile while getting Penny up, and then trailed the young girl downstairs and into the kitchen. Harry was there, just finishing his breakfast. Surprisingly, so was Margaret, still dressed in the satin nightgown that copied Mary's, barely covered by a negligé of lace and luminescence. They both looked up as the girls came in.

'Well, that was a surprise last night,' Harry boomed as he finished his cup. 'I thought you were spending the night with Penny. I'm sorry I was so tired.'

'Yes, I'm sure you were,' Mary said through stiff lips.

'And you must be feeling a bunch better, baby, if your mother could leave you in the middle of the night. Give us a kiss?'

Penny ran over to him, gave him a hug and kiss, and then pulled back from him. 'I do feel better,' she said, 'but you don't know Mommy. She wouldn't leave me in the middle of the night. She spent the whole night with *me*, Daddy. I think you must of goofed again!'

'She spent the whole——' He looked up at Mary's cold hard face, and turned red. 'You mean——' And then Margaret broke up, laughing so hard that she clutched at her stomach. A high shrill laugh, compounded of jealousy, hatred, and victory. When she recovered from her outburst she sat back in her chair, savouring her coffee, waiting.

'Mary?' There was a world of appeal in his voice, but it did not warm her, could not penetrate.

'Yes,' she said, 'I spent the night with Penny, except for a few minutes when I came to your room. Did you enjoy it?' She was whispering through half-closed lips, and a tear slowly trickled down one cheek. 'What is it with you? Some sort of challenge? To have *both* the McBain twins in the same week? How nice for your record!'

'Mary,' he snarled. 'Is this some kind of crazy game? What the hell is going on!'

'I thought that was *my* question,' she snapped back at him. 'But right now I have to talk to my sister. Why don't you get on your little tricycle and go make yourself another million dollars. Surely your ego has had a big enough boost during the night for that!'

Margaret was laughing again. Not the almost hysterical laugh she had displayed earlier, but a low gurgle of enjoyment. Penny looked around among the adults with a fearful expression on her face. It was not just what they were saying. The little girl was reading their feelings, and the tensions in the old kitchen were almost ceiling-high. 'You're *not* my Mommy's twin,' she sobbed, beating at Margaret with her little fists. 'She's beautiful. You're ugly! Ugly!' With a garbled sob she picked up the skirts of her robe and ran out of the room, crashing into the doorjamb on the way. Harry got up and rushed after her, muttering under his breath.

Mary watched them go, then turned back to her sister. 'Wait here,' she ordered in a cold commanding voice that startled them both. Margaret looked shaken as her sister stalked out into the hall. It took her five minutes for her to give her orders, and about ten to make the two telephone calls, then she came back to the kitchen.

Margaret, who had been slumped in her chair puffing madly at a cigarette, stood up nervously. Certainly in all her years she had never seen her older sister in such a condition as this.

'Upstairs and get dressed,' Mary grated.

'I intend to sit here and finish my breakfast, like any civilised person,' Margaret responded.

'The time for civilisation is over,' Mary snapped. 'We're finished being *lace-curtain* Irish, Margaret. We're back to *shanty* Irish, and old Southie!' She walked over to her twin sister, twisted the woman's arm around behind her back in a hammerlock, and forced her out of the kitchen and up the stairs. Mrs Hudley was in the bedroom when the two sisters came in.

'You're hurting me,' Margaret complained. 'What's she doing in my room?'

'I mean to hurt you. And if you give me any trouble I'll break your arm. She's packing. You get dressed.'

'You can't make me!'

Mary added an additional half inch to the pressure of her hold and stood wooden faced while her sister screamed. 'You still think I can't make you?' she asked softly.

'Okay. Okay,' Margaret sobbed. Mary dropped her punishing hold. Her sister rubbed her wrist to restore circulation, sobbing steadily. It's the first time I've ever heard Margaret cry, Mary told herself dispassionately. I wonder who she's crying for? Or what?

Margaret hurried, tossing dresses here and there as she fumbled her way into street clothes. Mary watched out the window until the cab drew up outside. 'Your time is up,' she said coldly.

'Up? What do you mean?'

'You're leaving my house,' Mary said softly. 'Right now. Bring the bag, Mrs Hudley.'

'I'm not going,' Margaret whined. But when Mary turned quickly on her, she backed away, frightened by the gleam in her sister's eye. 'All right, I'm going!'

'And that's for damn sure,' Mary muttered under her breath. On the landing Margaret managed to regain her aplomb, and strutted down the rest of the way to the front door as if it were all her own idea to leave. As Mary opened the door for her, Margaret sneered. 'Don't think this is the end of it. I'm not done with you—or Harry—yet!'

'Margaret, you'd do great in a 1910 melodrama,' Mary snarled, grabbing her sister's upper arm. 'But you'd better listen to me. If you come near me again, or even look crosswise at Harry, I'll take enough fingernails to you to make you look like Dracula's wife. Listen! I've made reservations for you at the Hilton. Harry will pay your bills for two weeks, and not another minute more. The rest of your luggage will be forwarded. And don't forget what I told you. Come back here, or meddle in *my* family, and your days as a beauty queen will be all over!'

'All right!' Margaret snarled. 'I don't know where you found the guts to do it, damn you. Goodbye, big sister.'

'Goodbye,' Mary said quietly. All her anger had drained out of her. She leaned back against the door and watched while her only direct blood relative hastened down the stairs, climbed into the taxi, and rode away. 'And I don't know where I got the guts to do it either,' she whispered to herself. Her hands were trembling in the aftermath of her ordeal. Mary McBain, the girl who wouldn't hurt a fly! But who could screw up her courage when someone dear to her was imperilled. Like Mother. Like Penny. Like—like Harry. And I only hope I've got the guts to do the harder part, she told herself as she made her way back into the house. Harry and his daughter were just coming out of the study as she started up the stairs.

'I'm going to take Penny to her eye appointment,' he said. 'I take it you've resolved the problem of too many McBain sisters?'

'Yes,' she retorted sharply. 'Yes I have.' She came back down the stairs to check Penny's dress, then knelt on the thick carpet and gave the little girl a death-hug and a tender kiss. 'Goodbye my lovely,' she said softly. 'I hope the doctor has good news, but good or not, your mother loves you. You understand?'

'I understand,' Penny whispered back. 'I love you too.' The pair of them went to the front door, hand in hand. Penny hesitated for a moment, before the door closed behind her, and stared with owl-eyes at her mother. Mary brushed a tear away from her own eyes and went upstairs to her room.

It took a half hour for her to pack her own bag, and to dress. She took only what was hers. Just the things she had brought into the house almost two months ago. Everything else—everything of his—she left hanging in the closet. She walked around the room when she had finished, touching the little things of his that were reminders. His hair brush. The one he hated to use because he thought he was losing his hair. His toothbrush in the bathroom. His pyjama bottoms, lying on the floor by the bed, as usual. She picked them up and tossed them into the laundry basket. Everything of his. And now she had to do the most difficult part. She picked up her bag and went down the stairs.

Stopping only long enough in the study to leave him a note about Margaret's hotel bills, she signed it 'Mary McBain'. What a long time ago it had been since he chased her around that desk, sandwich in hand and lust on his mind! So long ago. She had feared him then, in all her ignorance. Called him a devil to his face. And now there was a dull lump in the pit of her stomach, formed from all the love she bore for him. All the love which now must be torn out and discarded. With a bitter sigh she picked up the telephone and called the cab company.

Mrs Hudley was standing at the door as she went out. The elderly housekeeper had a bead of tears running down her cheek. 'Are you sure this is the only way?' she asked hopelessly.

'It's the only way.' Mary hugged her gently and kissed the parchment cheek. 'It's the only way I can see to free him from the McBain curse. I have to do it. He deserves more from life than what I have to give.'

'You know you love him,' the housekeeper said, reaching out a detaining hand.

'Yes, I know I love him,' she said bleakly. 'I only wish I knew if *he* loves—anyone.' She shook off the restraining hand, went down to the curb, and settled herself to wait for the cab.

It was a long ride, out Route Four westward, through historic Lexington—'where once the embattled farmers stood, and fired the shot heard round the world'—on past the Veterans Hospital, until they came to the tiny motel where she and her mother had once stopped. The cabbie waved aside her offer of payment. 'We bill Mr Richardson at the end of the month,' he said. 'Have a nice holiday.'

Have a nice holiday! The mockery followed her as she checked in, found her allotted room, locked the door behind her, and threw herself down on the bed. And then the tears came. In one's and two's, then dribbles, and rivulets, until she had cried out all her passions and fears, and thought she could face the lonely life ahead of her. At dinner time she managed the trip down the block to a local restaurant, and then went straight back to the motel.

She spent the evening worrying at her problem, like a puppy with an old bone. Assets? Good health, a teaching degree, two hundred dollars cash. Liabilities?

No job, *only* two hundred dollars, and—lord, I'm pregnant! Did I tell Harry? Well, he can only kill me once. Not much of a balance sheet. The summer vacation still had a week to run. Practically every community would have their teachers for the Fall semester already under contract. Elementary teachers were a dime a dozen! 'Why in the world didn't I major in maths or science?' she asked her mirror. 'There are always vacancies for maths teachers!'

How far would two hundred dollars take her? Not very. The little motel room cost twenty-two dollars a day. And—it's the household money that I took! I didn't think. He really *will* kill me for taking the household money! The incongruity of it struck her so hard that she dropped into the plastic chair and laughed until her stomach ached. He'd kill her for a good bit more than taking the household money—if ever he caught up with her. If ever he was *interested* in catching up with her. Too much! Her humour vanished, her spirits thumped down into her boots.

A shower should be the order of the day, she told herself. Well, at least it would pass a little time. She had barely opened her luggage when she checked in. Now she flipped through it for her toilet bag. Trailing the bag after her, she stumbled into the bathroom, sickening at the sanitary motel smell of the place.

Her clothes fell in a disorderly pile at her feet as she fished the hairpins out of her bun, and let her hair tumble down her back. She kicked the jumble of clothes out of the way and stepped into the shower stall, pulling the plastic curtain behind her. She soaped with enthusiasm, trying to wash her misery away, but no soap had ever been invented that was *that* strong. She shampooed her hair too, but no amount of scrubbing could relieve her mind. At last, clean but miserable, angry with herself and with the world, she shut off the water, grabbed up the minuscule towel provided by the management, and dried herself as best she could. When she had sopped off most of the water, she flung back the shower curtain, and backed out on to the bath mat. And into a pair of strong male arms!

She shrieked in alarm, a high quavering fearful scream. 'All right, Mary Richardson,' the voice in her ear grumbled, 'Haven't you given me enough trouble for one day?'

She forced her way out of his arms and scrabbled for the only remaining towel to cover her nudity. 'What—what are you doing here,' she shouted at him. 'You're in Boston!'

'Shut up,' he said gently. 'I'm not in Boston.'

'But you should be! Let me go! Put me down! Where's Penny?'

'Ah! It's about time we came to the important part. Penny's fine. And now that you've had your vacation, we're going home.'

'I am not,' she roared at him. 'I'm not going anywhere with you!'

'Don't tempt me, Miss Mary,' he said tolerantly. 'You've got a lovely bare bottom—that wants some whacking right now. Your towel is slipping.'

She did her best to remedy the deficiency, but the towel was just too small for the job. 'Put me down, you—you beast,' she yelled.

'That's the best idea yet,' he roared back at her. He was losing his temper. She cringed from the idea. If he really gets angry, she told herself, he will certainly do me some damage! She gave up the struggle, but it was too late to cool him down. He whipped her over his shoulder in a fireman's lift, hustled her out of the bathroom, and threw her down on the bed. She shrieked again as the bed bounced beneath her, and lost her towel completely.

He stood at the foot of the bed and glowered at her. 'Now I warn you, Miss Mary,' he said, 'I've had it up to here. Get yourself dressed. You're coming with me!'

'Don't look at me like that,' she snapped, doing her best to cover her breasts from his devouring stare.

'Don't look at you like what?'

'Lust!' she shouted at him. 'Don't look at me like— that.'

'Love!' he shouted back at her. 'Can't you tell the difference?'

'No, I can't,' she screamed back. 'And neither could you last night! What are you, some kind of comparison shopper?'

'Damn you, woman, I've already made my pick. I want you! I love you! And nothing happened last night. Nothing! I was too damn tired. And I told you so—I mean, I told Margaret so! Get dressed!'

'That's a damn likely story,' she said bitterly. 'The wolf of Charles Street, and nothing happened? If anyone believes that I'd like to sell them the Brooklyn bridge. And I'm *not* getting dressed. I will not go anywhere with you, you hear?'

'Yes, I hear. And so do half the other people in this stupid motel. Get dressed!'

'I will not! How did you find me?'

'Mary, if I didn't love you so much I would call you dumb! Dumb, dumb, dumb! What other woman in the world would run away from her husband using his own taxicab company? I just called the dispatcher. What else? Get dressed!'

He hadn't touched Margaret? Who could believe that? Besides me, that is. I love you. He keeps saying that. I love you—I made my pick! She swallowed her anger and despondency, but not her independence. 'I'm not going with you,' she said in a tiny lost voice. 'I won't get dressed.'

'Okay, that does it,' he roared at her. Before she could make a defensive move he whipped the top blanket up around her, doing her up into a neat package, with both arms and legs confined, and threw her over his shoulder again.

'What are you doing to me,' she screamed in real terror.

'I'm taking my wife home,' he shouted back. He picked up her suitcase in his free hand. The latch was not shut, so it tumbled open. 'To hell with it,' he muttered, and stalked out the door, leaving her clothing scattered across the floor. A half-dozen people from neighbouring rooms were clustered together on the walk. He gave them all a big smile. 'FBI,' he called cheerily. 'I've finally got her. Bonnie Parker, the outlaw!' He patted her very convenient bottom proprietorially. 'She specialises in bank jobs.'

'Yeah, I seen that on television the other night,' one of the ladies said excitedly. 'Her and that guy Clyde. Wow!'

'He's kidnapping me,' Mary shouted from the depths of the blanket. 'Help! He's kidnapping me!' One of the women in the crowd laughed nervously. One of the bigger men settled the confusion.

'Well, they can't get away with it forever. Want me to hold the car door? Have a good night.'

Have a good night, indeed, she thought bitterly, as he tossed her into the front seat. Male chauvinism. Have a good night! What am I, some kind of harem slave? Harry walked around the hood, climbed in, pushed the starter button, and drove off. She huddled in the corner, not exactly sure how angry he was. After a few miles she ventured a gambit. 'Where are we going?'

'Home.'

'Home? You're driving west, away from the city.'

'Of course I am. The city's no place to raise a family. We bought a house in Concord about four weeks ago.'

'A home in Concord? Why?'

'The next time I buy a wife I'm going to be more careful about checking the operating instructions. Now, just listen up. Next Thursday week—what day is that?'

'September, oh I don't know! Why do you bother—oh dear. It's my birthday.'

'Yes. So I bought you a birthday present. A house in the country! And I've been working all out to get it fixed up. That's how come I was so tired when I got home yesterday.'

'A likely story,' she said softly. 'I'm cold.'

'Well, you had your chance to put your clothes on.

Now you'll either suffer in silence, or cuddle up. Take your pick.'

'You could turn on the car heater.'

'No I couldn't. I gave you your choice, now shut up.'

She managed to bounce halfway across the wide seat, but hesitated over the last few inches. The blanket kept slipping. 'This is a terrible way to treat a pregnant lady,' she commented.

'You didn't get that way all by yourself,' he snapped. She tried to search his face, but the highway was unlit, and the occasional gleam of moonlight failed to penetrate. I'll have to move closer to see if he's angry, she told herself. And it seemed to be so logical an excuse that she slid across the intervening space and found her head on his warm shoulder, her leg against his, her arms in his lap, the whole of her surrounded by the one arm he could spare from the steering wheel.

'That's better,' he gruffed. 'Admit that you're whipped?'

'I—no such a thing,' she stammered. He shifted his left hand down on the wheel, and pulled her closer to him.

'Give up while it's graceful,' he prodded. 'You happen to be my woman. My only woman, and I intend to keep you on ball and chain until its suits my fancy to do otherwise. And I'm very glad that you're pregnant. You left the letter on the hall table.'

'Yes,' she sighed, confessed everything with that one brief exhalation. Didn't it sound terrible? His woman. Ball and chain! It sounded—'If that's what is on offer,' she said quietly, 'I accept.'

Penny ran down the steps of their new house, and pulled open the car door. 'Mommy!' she squealed, forcing her way inside the car and on to Mary's lap. 'Lookit! They gave me new glasses. I can see—well, not everything, but most. Only I don't know how to read, Mommy. Isn't this a wonderful house. Daddy said you went on a vacation. I'm glad it's over!'

'Hey,' he cautioned. 'Your mother has had a hard

day. And don't worry about learning to read. We have our very own teacher in the family.'

'Mommy? You're only wearing a blanket! Remember when you first came to our house, and you didn't have no nightgown? Did you and Daddy get married again?'

'Now that's the best question I've heard tonight.' He looked over the child's head and gave Mary a wicked smile. 'Yes, your mom and I have just got married again. Now, which one of you shall I carry into the house?'

'You can't carry us both?' Penny teased.

'No I can't,' he said. 'Not without using up all my strength so that I'll be too tired to do anything else tonight.'

'I'll walk,' Mary returned. 'Go ahead. I'll walk.'

The steps up to the old-fashioned porch were freshly mended. The house gleamed with a new coat of paint, its windows countersigned with solid wooden shutters. Mrs Hudley was waiting at the door, smiling, and behind her a well-lit hall, with a magnificent set of mahogany stairs in the background.

'Built in 1807,' he boasted as he set Penny down. 'And I did most of the repair work myself.'

'Dinner in half an hour?' Mrs Hudley suggested.

'You'd better make that an hour,' he answered. 'And now you, lady!' Mary pulled her blanket tightly around her and wondered what was coming next. He still looked mean enough to—well—that was the question, wasn't it? He wasted no words. She was swept up in his arms and carried up the stairs. His foot kicked a bedroom door open.

'The master suite,' he announced. He carried her over to the massive Emperor-sized bed, and dropped her into the middle of it. She bounced a couple of times, then struggled to sit up.

'Come on,' he growled. 'We need a shower.'

She climbed off the bed reluctantly, pushing her feet into a pair of slippers that had been half-hidden under the bed. He walked off towards the bathroom. She scurried to follow. 'You fixed this all up?' she called after him. 'The stairs, the paint, the bathroom?'

'You bet,' he snapped. 'The stairs were easy. The paint just took time. But the bathroom—well, I had to do it over three times, and the third time I called in a plumber to supervise. No remarks, now. Inside!'

'I—I wasn't going to say——' Her fist plugged up her mouth. Without waiting for her at all he had calmly taken off all his clothes, and stood magnificently naked before her in the full brightness of the lights. She took a deep breath, unable to take her eyes from him, and her blanket slipped to the floor. He turned his back to her to adjust the temperature of the shower water, than looked at her over his shoulder.

'Look at you,' he laughed, 'all tousled and naked. Lovely, Mrs Richardson.'

'I am not naked,' she protested. 'I'm wearing my slippers, and that's more than you are wearing!' Oh lord, she muttered, half to herself. Let me learn to keep my big mouth shut! He's laughing at me—just a little bit. Maybe he doesn't mean to kill me dead. Maybe, if I handle it right, we might be able to get back on an even keel? But—what do I know about seducing my husband?

He stepped into the shower stall and ducked under the spray, sending a sprinkle of warm water at her. She stood and watched, bewitched. So big! With broad shoulders, tapering down to a narrow waist and hips. Muscles everywhere, bronzed by the sun except for that narrow band normally covered by his trunks. And narrow muscled flanks, outlined in pale white against the bronze of the rest of him. And he wanted her! That's something a man couldn't hide. 'Come on in,' he coaxed, 'the water's fine!'

She plucked up her courage and stepped in. The water blinded her for a moment. She clutched at him for support.

'If you're going to do that,' he yelled over the roar of the water, 'use some soap!' She grabbed up a bar of perfumed soap from the dish, stretched up on tiptoes, and began scrubbing his back, running her hands from his shoulders down past his hips, down each of his legs. She knelt down in front of him to reach his ankles and his feet.

'That's the way it should be,' he laughed down at her. 'My loving wife, on her knees! Up you come, shorty, it's your turn.'

'Don't you dare call me shorty,' she snapped. But her heart wasn't in it. By that time he had pulled her up and back against his hard wet frame, and was busy swathing her with suds. It was a warm, comfortable feeling as he laved her back, and then rinsed her off. But when his soapy slippery fingers reached around and began to massage her hips, her stomach, the line of her rib-cage, and then lingered longingly on the full undercurves of her breasts, it became sheer torment—and she told him so. Which earned only a laugh as his hands dropped lower to soap her thighs.

'Okay,' he finally called. 'Stay under the water for a minute.' He stepped out and towelled himself vigorously. Stay under the water, she asked herself? Good lord, how can I calmly stand under the flow of this water when he—and he knows it, too! Nevertheless she managed to remain under the deluge, holding her mass of wet hair clear of her face so she could watch him— devour him—with her eyes. And then he extended a hand and drew her out on to the rug.

He smothered her in towels, gently drying her hair, her back, her legs. And then once again he pulled her back against him and began that sensual massage that so aroused her. Somewhere in the transition the towels were lost. She could feel the tension of his aroused muscles playing against her back. Until finally it all went beyond her control. 'Now! Please!' she pleaded.

He picked her up in his arms and carried her back to the giant bed, dropping her in the middle of it, and falling beside her as she fell. His hands wandered again, down across her stomach, and farther. His questing tongue tantalised her taut nipples until she squirmed against him, urging him, compelling him. And now it was not a case of him taking her. Rather they met as equals on the field of love, smashed at each other in eager anticipation, until they achieved a wonderous union, and then lay panting in each other's arms.

It seemed like hours that they lay together, satiated. Her head was tucked under his chin, her cheek rubbing against the relaxed muscles of his chest. His one hand threaded the soft silk of her hair. The other rested comfortable under the curve of her tender swollen breast.

'You know what?' she said. He grunted. 'When I first met you—that first night on Joy Street—I thought you were the devil himself, come to claim me. And I didn't even know your name. Remember?'

'I remember. I thought you were the most beautiful woman in the world!'

'Baloney! you couldn't tell me from Margaret. You *still* can't! Are you positive nothing happened when—that was a pretty thin excuse, you know!'

'That's the trouble when you use the truth as an excuse,' he chuckled. 'I can think of a much better story. You want one?'

'I—no. I would rather believe what you told me. I *do* believe you. I *do* believe you!'

His roaming hand pulled at a tendril of her hair. 'Keep saying that, over and over. I believe everything Harry tells me. I believe everything Harry tells me!'

'Well I do,' she said angrily. 'Everything! Only how come a millionaire banker has to fix up his own house. And be so damned rushed about it?'

'I needed the exercise,' he said solemnly. 'Do you remember when I first carried you up the stairs at Joy Street? I was out of puff by the third step. I couldn't have made the second floor if my life depended on it. So, it was either an exercise programme at the YMCA, or the house. I picked the house. And as for rushing— well, I wanted it ready for your birthday. It's in your name, you know. And then—Penny has to go to school in September, and I meant to finish here so that she could start her new school in Concord. Hey, I admit it was ambitious, but once I got caught up in the programme, I had to finish it. Do you believe that?'

'Of course I do.' She sighed reflectively. 'Who could invent a lie as stupid as that?' She dropped a kiss on his chin. 'But do you suppose Margaret will be all right?'

'I'm sure she will,' he assured her gently. 'When her money runs out I'll offer her a job as assistant manager for one of my hotels in London. I think she'd make a marvellous hostess.' One of his hands idly climbed the mound of her breast and squeezed the nipple.

'Hey, that hurts,' she complained.

'What's the matter? Can't stay the course?'

'You—you bit me before—you devil! You bit me. It's sore.'

'What did you expect? You were a wildcat. Is that what they teach elementary schoolteachers?'

'No!' she snapped, and then burst out laughing. 'Nobody taught me. You're the only man I ever wanted. Ever since that morning when you came back with that finagled marriage licence. And you treat me like a—madman!'

'How do you want to be treated?'

She slipped away from his arms, stretched out on her back, and smiled through half-closed eyes. 'Like Cleopatra,' she whispered. 'I'm the queen of Egypt, being rowed up the Nile, the moon is shining, and there are flowers all over the boat. Julius Caesar is coming up on the quarter deck, and——'

'Wait just one minute, Cleo,' he laughed, 'I have to get out of my armour!'

Two days later the three of them came up to the city to make arrangements about Penny's school records. After concluding their business at Court Street, he drove them down to City Hall Plaza. For once his phenomenal luck failed him. He couldn't find a parking space. 'Watch your language,' she cautioned, 'there are ladies and children present.'

'Oh shut up,' he grumped, as he finally squeezed into a *No Parking* zone down by the Quincy Market. 'I've got business at City Hall,' he announced.

'We'll walk over with you,' Mary suggested hopefully. Although the weather had turned, she had no desire to sit in an over-heated car while he negotiated his business. He didn't answer, but she philosophically decided that since he hadn't said no, he must mean yes. She towed a giggling Penny out of the car and they pursued him over the vast paved expanse in front of Faneuil Hall. By the time they reached the tiny park, the only grassed area in sight, with its scattered trees looking cool in the late afternoon breeze, Penny had had enough.

'We'll wait for you here,' Mary yelled after him. He waved a hand but kept going. 'Sit down here on this bench,' Mary suggested. The little girl, her glasses perched on the tip of her nose, drew back.

'There's something sitting there, Mommy,' she muttered.

Mary turned around to look, and laughed. 'There certainly is,' she giggled finally. 'But he doesn't mind sharing. Go take a close look, love.'

'But he's a strange man,' Penny whispered fiercely. 'You know I ain't supposed to talk to strange men!'

'He's the strangest man you'll ever meet, and it's perfectly okay when your mother is here.' Mary sat down at one end of the bench, and gave Penny a small shove towards the other end. A man sat there casually, one leg crossed over the other, one arm along the back of the bench, surveying the centre of the city. And then Penny squealed. 'He's not real! He's a statue, or something, made out of metal.'

'Of course he is, love. His name was James Michael Curley. He was mayor of our city for a long time.' Penny edged her way back, her eyes still on the statue. James Michael, Mary mused. The last of the big city bosses in Boston. The man who ruled the city between the two World Wars. The last of the Irish politicians, who gave way to the later immigrants, the Italians, the Greeks, the Latinos. But there he sat, memorialised by the citizens in bronze.

Across the area over which they had walked a crowd

was gathering, lighted candles in hand, for some sort of open-air protest meeting in front of Faneuil Hall. Closer, a group of saffron-dressed men were making their way towards a gaggle of tourists. And just to the right of the beggars—'Hey Penny, look!'

'Look at what?'

'The policeman. The one with the horse. Don't you remember him?'

'No I don't.' Harry returned at that moment and sat down with them, whistling happily. 'That's Officer Timulty, the policeman who gave us our accident at the State House. Remember?'

'Oh, him.' The little girl was disinterested, her eyes on the more brightly dressed beggars.

'Boy what a spoilsport,' Mary groaned. 'Did you finish your business, dear?'

'Yes. It didn't take long. It was about your father's safe deposit box. I had to sign an affidavit that it was empty when the FBI man and I opened it.'

'Empty?' She looked up at him with love in her eyes. 'Was it?' He nodded. 'Why you big fake,' she laughed. 'Then if it was empty when the FBI looked, how come Margaret found twenty thousand dollars in it? How come?'

'Well——' he stalled. 'So all right. I got tired of having her around the house, but I couldn't have my sister-in-law walking the streets, could I? It was worth it.'

'What's that mean,' Penny asked. 'Walking the streets?'

'That means—er—walking the streets—like the policeman does,' Mary lied.

'That don't sound right,' the child commented. And she's got her teeth in it now, Mary told herself, and she won't let go without a diversion.

'Come on, Penny,' she said, grabbing the child's hand. 'We owe a lot to Officer Timulty, and now's our chance to thank him.'

'For knocking us both down? For that he needs thanks?'

'Come on!' She pulled the girl up, and they started across the plaza in the direction of the dismounted officer, who was lazily watching the group of beggars.

Harry followed slowly behind them, grinning.

'Officer,' Mary yelled as they closed in on him. 'Officer Timulty!' He shifted the reins of his horse to his other hand and turned towards her. His youthful face turned a dozen colours in succession.

'Oh no,' he groaned. 'Not you! Have you come to bite me again?' He stepped back a couple of paces, away from the threat.

'No,' she called. 'We've come to thank you.'

'Have you blown your mind again, lady? Thank me for what?'

'For everything!' she exclaimed in a gleefully loud voice. Naturally, in the open Plaza, she drew the attention of a group of on-lookers. 'I *have* to thank you,' she repeated. 'Look, this is my daughter Penny.'

'Please lady, don't make a fuss,' he returned. 'I know you have a thing against me, but after all, I'm the one who got bitten.'

'I'm not angry,' Mary returned. 'Honest. Look at Penny. She was blind until you—until your horse knocked her down. And now she can see. Isn't that wonderful?'

'Yeah, wonderful.' He shook his head, confused.

'And look at me! I'm pregnant, and I owe it all to you!'

The officer backed off a couple more steps, putting himself almost into the Mayor's bronze lap. 'I didn't have nothing to do with that, lady,' he said sharply. 'You can't tell me that knocking you down made you——' Harry came up to his rescue, putting his arm around each of his ladies.

'She's my wife,' Harry said. 'And I am solely responsible for her pleasant condition.' There was a smattering of applause from the gathering audience. A voice in the rear of the crowd yelled, 'Police Brutality!'

The policeman moved closer to his horse. 'You're wife is a crazy,' he said hoarsely. 'I didn't have anything to do with her being pregnant!' Which was just the moment Penny and Mary chose to surround him, kissing him on each blushing cheek. He threw up his hands in self-defence, too late.

'I don't know how you can stand being married to that one,' he finally ground out. 'She takes the cake!'

'She does indeed,' Harry assured him happily. 'Every night. Why did you kiss the policeman, Miss Mary?'

'The devil made me do it,' she said demurely.

He patted her bottom, and escorted both of them back to the car. Inside, she turned to him with an appeal in her eyes. 'Do you ever think I can become the wife you want? One with poise and guts?'

'You have already arrived, my dear,' he said quietly. 'The day you threw Margaret out of our house was your graduation day.' He started the engine of the car.

'Invited her to leave,' Mary insisted. 'Not threw her out—invited her to leave.' He patted her knee and started the car in motion.

'My goodness you two are funny,' Penny said happily from the seat between them.

Officer Timulty, deciding that he would let the beggars get away with their act, swung himself back up into the saddle and watched the big car move away. He pushed his cap back and scratched his forehead. 'What is the world coming to?' he asked his horse.

James Michael Curley, cast in bronze, just smiled out at the city he had loved. And why not? After all, he had seen the same story replayed a thousand times over in Beantown.

An epic novel of exotic rituals
and the lure of the Upper Amazon

THE TAKERS
RIVER OF GOLD

JERRY AND S.A. AHERN

THE TAKERS are the intrepid Josh Culhane and the
seductive Mary Mulrooney. These two adventurers
launch an incredible journey into the Brazilian rain
forest. Far upriver, the jungle yields its deepest
secret—the lost city of the Amazon warrior women!

THE TAKERS series is making publishing history.
Awarded *The Romantic Times* first prize for High
Adventure in 1984, the opening book in the series
was hailed by *The Romantic Times* as "the next
trend in romance writing and reading. Highly
recommended!"

Jerry and S.A. Ahern have never been better!

TAK – 3

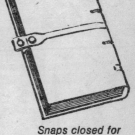